LUCID DREAMERS

THE LUCIDERS

LUCID DREAMERS

THE LUCIDERS

R.D. JOHNSON JR.

Two Harbors Press
212 3rd Avenue North, Suite 290
Minneapolis, MN 55401
612.455.2293
www.TwoHarborsPress.com

ISBN-13: 978-1-937928-58-2
LCCN: 2012937068

Distributed by Itasca Books

Cover Design by Alan Pranke
Typeset by James Arneson

Printed in the United States of America

I dedicate this book to my fiancée, Arlene, for believing in me and encouraging me to write down my thoughts. She is my link between my reality and my dream, merging them into one.

ACKNOWLEDGMENTS

To my children, Brandon, BreAnn, Ciera, and Dustin: I want you to know your dreams will come true as long as you believe in yourselves and continue to search for and live your dreams. It is when you desire to combine dreams with reality that you truly will live.

To my parents, Harold and Nancy, and my sisters, Patricia, Coreena, and Barbara: thank you for standing by me and providing support not only in my dreams but also through my nightmares.

PROLOGUE

Dreams are what make us, and we are what make our dreams. If we have life, we also have dreams. So I ask, if life as we know it suddenly disappeared, how would we know it? By living every second of our lives.

Dreams. We have them when we sleep, when we think of our future, and even as we ponder what's next in our lives. They lie in shadows, waiting, anticipating our appearance as they seize our very essences between the dark and the light, preventing us from escaping their grasp, not just in their domain but ours as well.

Slipping through the shroud that separates their world from ours, dreams reach out as violently as lightning strikes in dark clouds, snatching our being into their clutches. We find ourselves abruptly in their sphere of influence, while we're taken through the corridors of the unknown, passing the boundaries of reason and understanding.

They take us farther across the expanse, where we find ourselves imprisoned on the other side of emptiness—for a moment, hours, or a lifetime, trying to comprehend their world as they give us insight to sights and sounds that are strange to us.

As we float among their worlds, we're at their mercy, while visions of the unknown and the familiar are shown to us, telling stories. We question if it's one of beauty, where our heart yearns to return, or nightmarish, where we're caged in a world as they taunt us.

After they've done their will without sympathy, they release us from the spells of hope or discouragement, as the visions fade from view. From their liberation, they send us from their world, watching as we drift through the darkness, back through the veil into our world.

For some of us, their cruelty is hard to understand, as we wake up lost in thoughts of how great life would be if we could stay there, living as we wish, while others of us have nightmares from which we can't escape, and there is anger and resentment as we open our eyes to the world in which we live.

A world within a world, dreams create their own reality by putting us in situations over which we have no control. Some say dreams are release mechanisms, providing rest from our daily lives, while others say the dream is reality and reality is the dream. And still others believe our dream is someone else's reality, and our reality is someone else's dream.

Have you thought of something right before you slept, and it continued on in a dream? Or have you wakened from a dream, only to find similarities in reality? And what of those dreams we wake from and want to go back to sleep to finish or change the outcome? Does that mean dreams and reality are just extensions of each other, and we haven't figured a way to merge the two?

What about dying? If we die in a dream, do we also die in reality? What about waking up? If we wake up from a dream and know we have dreamed, why couldn't we wake up inside a dream and know we're dreaming? If death in one brings death in the other, why couldn't life in one bring life to the other?

If we could live in dreams alongside reality and be conscience of both, would we be able to tell them apart?

My friends and I no longer wonder why something happens in dreams, nor do we wish we could go back to sleep to change the outcome. We're no longer concerned with similarities between dreams and reality. To us, dreams and reality are the same, only separated by sleep or wakefulness, depending on one's perspective.

We've discovered that since we have multiple lives in reality, we also have many lives in our dreams. And we've found how to live in our dreams the same way we live in reality. And after choosing the life we live, regardless of whether it's reality or a dream, we're stuck with that life until we consciously or unintentionally change its course.

I'm David Birch. I'm a senior at the local high school. What separates me from other kids is that I'm able to control my dreams when I go to sleep. I know that may not sound very exciting, but think about it: when you wake up from a dream, you may or may not remember it. And instead of participating actively in your dreams, you just go along until you wake up.

Realizing you're in a dream and having the ability to control it not only is a way to enjoy the dream but also is a way for you to do whatever you want inside it. You can go anywhere, see anyone, be anyone, or even try different outcomes. If you don't like it, change it. What a great way to spend a good night's sleep.

In addition to my learning to control my dreams, some of my friends also have the gift. In our dreams, we will meet at some place we've decided upon in reality, usually the pond at the local park. And we do what teenagers do best: doing what we want. Before I tell you our story and how our dreams turned out, I'll let my friends introduce themselves. ...

I'm Raelen—my friends call me Rae—and I'm also a senior. David and I have been going to the same schools since elementary. I didn't believe I could control my dreams until one night I saw David and I—

Hey, you're giving the story away.

Fine. I won't tell them. Anyway, before David interrupted me, I was saying that I, too, control my dreams.

Hey, I'm Bobby, and when I found out I could control my dreams, I jumped on the idea of living in a world I created—even though I have to go to sleep to enjoy it. Fortune and fame in reality can't even touch the fun I have in dreams. Kicking back and enjoying my dreams is a great way to spend a night. And I will tell you this: it sucks waking up from a good dream.

I'm Steve, and I'm seventeen. After discovering what I could do in dreams, I've reached the point where I'd rather stay in my dreams than face reality. At least in my dreams, I'm safe.

Well, there you have it—

Excuse me? I'm part of this group too.

Oh, yeah. Rae's little sister, Mary, learned about dreams when she was spying on Rae and me.

You don't want me to tell them about your story, so let me tell them who I am.

Hi, everyone, I'm Mary, Raelen's *younger* sister, not little as someone would want you to believe. I'm going on thirteen.

But thinks she's eighteen.

I can still tell Dad you were kissing, David, instead of watching me, if you interrupt me again.

Okay, brat, go and finish.

I enjoy going into dream world, that's what I call it. But it's the running from—oops. Sorry. I'm not supposed to talk about what happens. But you know who I am.

As I was saying, my friends and I—and, of course, Mary— have learned to control our dreams. As a joke, we were going to call ourselves the Dream Kids, but Mary said she wasn't a baby goat. This is the beginning of our story, and we are the Luciders.

CHAPTER 1 DREAM REALITY

"No, not now!" I said after hearing a ringing sound as I flew behind Rae like a bird, gliding through the woods, across the snowy peaks of mountains, trying to beat her to the finish line somewhere in the valley below. As we raced, the pine trees that stood as spikes rising from the earth started bending over from the force that shot out from our hands, creating a path deeper into the forest.

As I gained speed, my heart raced rapidly when I saw Rae flying into a dark cavern, shouting incantations that illuminated the crystal walls inside and echoed throughout the mountains outside. As I flew behind her, I could see the glow that shone around her as she dashed left to right and right to left, avoiding the stalactites and stalagmites that formed the teeth of the cavern beast, leaving shadows on the walls as she rushed past them.

When we approached the end of the cave inside the mountain, rays of light broke through, revealing our way out of the creature. Then we soared from its mouth, shouting and laughing as we rose above the canopy of trees. As we soared past the last summit that rose above the earth, I could see Rae's long, thick, brunette hair flying in the wind just ahead of me as we started our descent, falling like stars crossing the universe as we flew toward the vale.

I heard the ringing again, and I knew I was running out of time. I tried to catch her at the base of the mountains where the swamp rolled from the hillsides, creating a shimmering blanket from the sunrays upon the valley. Flying above the cattails that sprang forth from the marsh, I made my final thrust, and we flew neck-and-neck when we came out of the mire, heading toward our destination.

With plush grass beneath us, we flew faster, leaving a wake of wind behind. Each of us was determined to beat the other and gain the victory when we both saw the end of our flight just ahead. But I saw my triumph slowly dissolve when Rae flew past me, smiling … just as I opened my eyes after hearing the alarm clock remind me of the world I'd just left.

"Damn," I said quietly, feeling disappointed. As I lay on my bed staring up at the ceiling, I wondered why I'd set the alarm on a Sunday morning. Still feeling the coolness of the breeze from the mountains on my face, I lay there wishing I could go back to sleep and start again. Once again I'd been taken from the world I'd grown accustomed to, leaving me in a reality that didn't compare to the dreams I enjoyed night after night.

I got up and looked out the window, glancing at the frost-covered rooftops that lined the streets. On this early spring morning, I wondered if the people inside those houses were feeling as alive as I did. Or did they wake up, not knowing the life they left behind? Did they miss the beauty of their dreams, not knowing they could have taken control of each aspect of their dreams? I knew only one thing for certain: dreamers were waking up to either control their dreams … or be controlled by them.

I got dressed and headed downstairs for something to eat. Thinking about how I almost beat Rae in our flying dream, I was humming as I walked into the kitchen.

"You're in a good mood," my mom said, smiling as she handed me a plate of food.

"I've traveled the world, sailed the seas, and soared through mountains. I've created life, and I've changed life," I told her. "And now, I have the world in my hands to mold and make it as I see fit." I grinned, feeling alive because I'd found the gift of dreams.

My mother looked at me with a puzzled expression. "What are you talking about?"

"Nothing," I responded, taking my seat at the kitchen table.

Wendy, my nine-year-old sister, was already sitting there, eating her breakfast.

"Why are you guys up early on Sunday?" I asked, wondering why Mom had breakfast already prepared.

She gave me a strange look. "This is Monday, not Sunday."

"Yeah, right," I said, thinking she was teasing me. When I checked the calendar and realized she was correct, I felt lost in time—and confused. "I could have sworn today was Sunday," I said quietly.

"Eat your breakfast," my mother advised. "That should help. You had a rough night last night."

I didn't respond; I just sat there, trying to remember what I'd done last night.

"David, are you okay?" Mom said as I sat lost in thought.

"I'm okay," I responded with a half-smile.

"Good," she said. "And remember, you have chores to finish up tonight after school that you didn't finish yesterday." Then she shouted for Tommy, my fourteen-year-old brother, to hurry up and get downstairs.

I couldn't remember if I'd done any chores the day before, but now I was thinking about my graduation, which was only a few months away. "After school?" I repeated. "That's almost a thing of the past. I live in the future; that's where my dreams are—the future."

My family always ate breakfast together unless my dad was out of town on business, and that was usually in the middle of the week. Because he hadn't joined us at the table, I asked Wendy, "Where's Dad?"

Wendy gave me a blank stare and then looked as if she was about to cry.

Tommy came into the kitchen and said, "Dad? What do you mean, 'Dad'?" He had an unpleasant tone in his voice.

"Yes, Dad. Where is he?" I shot back, annoyed by the tone of his voice and expression on his face.

Tommy sat down across from me, rolled his eyes, shook his head, and sneered. "You really do have issues, don't you?"

"What's your problem?" I asked. I looked at my mom, and her expression was similar to Wendy's sad face. "Mom, why are you looking like that?" I asked.

"Sweetie, are you sure you're okay this morning?" Her voice was gentle, but she continued to stare at me with worried look. I couldn't understand the sudden change in everyone's mood.

"No, he's not okay," Tommy said. "He's going crazy again." Tommy made gestures with his face and hands to indicate my mental state, and then he started laughing at me.

Mom slammed down a spoon on the kitchen counter. "Stop it, Tommy!" she shouted furiously. Her face started turning red with rage and her hands started shaking.

I was startled by her outburst and quickly got up from the table to go to her, trying to understand why tears were forming in her eyes.

I stood there, thinking the worst and getting a queasy feeling. I looked at my siblings and then back to Mom and asked in a shaky, solemn voice, "What is the matter?" She turned away from me, wiping her tears. "Mom?" I said, trying to get her to look at me. And then a thought came to mind. "Mom," I said again, my voice trembling with uncertainty, "Is Dad okay?"

She seemed unable to speak clearly but finally choked out, "David ... don't do this." She leaned against the counter, trembling.

"Don't do what?" I asked, not understanding.

She turned and stared into my eyes, as if she was reaching deep into my soul, searching for something that wasn't there.

She took a deep breath and exhaled slowly. "You know how this upsets Wendy," she said, her voice suddenly stern. "So just drop it!"

I shook my head in amazement at how things were going. "Okay, I'm confused. What's the joke?" I was trying to lighten the mood—but then Mom slapped my face.

"Stop talking like that!" she screamed as I rubbed the burning feeling she left on my cheek.

Wendy started shouting, "I hate you! I hate you!" and ran out of the kitchen, crying.

Tommy stood up, knocking over the chair he'd been sitting in. "Joke?" he exploded. "So now you think it's a *joke*?" Tommy shoved past me toward the kitchen door.

"Shut the hell up," I said as he walked past me. My confusion was turning to anger.

Tommy turned around long enough to say, "You're an ass," before he stormed out of the kitchen.

I started to go after him, but my mom shrieked loudly enough to be heard throughout the house. "Enough! That's *enough*!" Her face was red from shouting, as she'd tried to control the situation.

I tried desperately to collect my thoughts and calm down. I felt sympathetic to her emotions as she began to cry. "Mom, what's going on?" I asked, begging for an answer.

She sat down at the table and rested her forehead in her hands, covering her face. "Sweetie, I'm exhausted. I can't handle this anymore," she said, trying to speak between crying and sniffling.

"Exhausted?" I asked. "Exhausted from what?" I walked over to the table as I tried to figure out how the morning that had started so good could now bring such pain. I sat across from her, waiting for an answer.

She took another deep breath and said, "We can do this." She spoke softly, trying to smile, and wiped her eyes. "We can do this." She looked up at me, taking my hands in hers.

I suddenly felt scared for what she might tell me, but I had to know.

"Do what, Mom?" My heart started pounding harder with each second that she hesitated to speak.

Her sweaty hands tightly gripped mine as she said slowly, "Every couple of months we go through this."

I sat there thinking about what had happened a couple of months ago. I was still confused. "Go through what?"

I watch her grasp at the right words to say. She tried to maintain eye contact with me and finally said in a sorrowful voice, "A relapse."

I sat there with my eyes opened wide, feeling helpless. "A … what?" I asked, not believing what I had just heard.

"David, you're having a relapse," she replied sadly. She pressed her lips tightly together, as if she didn't want to say the word again.

I didn't know if I should laugh or tell her she was crazy, but the words I was trying to speak didn't come out; I just sat there as the word "relapse" echoed in my mind.

"David …" she said, breaking the silence around us, "you were diagnosed with grandiose delusional disorder."

"I don't know what you mean," I said. "What's that?" I posed the question with skepticism, not believing something was wrong with me.

"Grandiose delusional disorder—it has to do with a person having delusions about identity, among other delusions." She looked very serious as she held back more tears.

As I shook my head again, avoiding her eyes, my body took over on its own, forcing me to chuckle at her words.

"David, it's not funny. You're having a relapse. I guess I need to call Dr. Maiden to have your medication increased again."

"My medication? I don't take any medicine." I spoke loudly, sure of myself as I took control of my thoughts.

"Just drop it," she said, sounding irritated.

"Who the hell is Dr. Maiden, and what do you mean relapse and medicine?" I shouted, raising my voice because I wasn't getting the answers I needed.

"Dr. Maiden is your psychiatrist. You've been seeing him for a year now. And according to the doctor, some teenagers, especially boys your age, experience this type of behavior when a loved one dies, especially their dad. The boys believe they have to step in and take over in the family." She began weeping and speaking of things I wasn't aware of. "You're on prescription medication that helps you cope, so you don't have to feel you need to take your dad's place. And when you don't keep up with your medicine, you have a relapse."

As I sat there with my mouth open, I wondered if I had heard her correctly. "What the hell did you just say?" My throat felt like it was tightening, almost causing me to hyperventilate as I waited for her to answer.

She held my hands, and I could feel her sweaty palms squeezing harder. Her words seemed to be strangled in her throat, preventing them from escaping from her dry mouth.

"David," she finally said, "you know that your father has been dead for over a year now ..."

I saw her mouth move; she was forming words that I couldn't hear or comprehend. I sat there, unable to move the muscles in my body as I thought about how much I wanted to run away—anywhere—as my heartbeat began getting louder. Her lips seemed to move in slow motion. Each second felt like an hour, and I felt myself shrieking from inside my dull, numb body, which barely kept me sitting upright in the chair.

I knew this wasn't happening, but I was unable to control the world that was just given to me. As I looked around the room, trying to get my bearings, walls, counters, windows, doors—everything in the kitchen, even the table and chair where I was sitting—started fading. I felt myself being lifted to another world inside my mind. I looked for shadows to hide in, as each moment cruelly pierced my soul, leaving me to bleed in the anguish of my body.

As I continued in my mind, floating from one time to another, trying frantically to grasp something that was real to hold onto and believe in, I could feel my body somewhere on the outside of me, tightening around my spirit, laughing as it continued choking me, keeping my breath from escaping and leaving me to live the same breath over and over.

Steadily, I began to hear her words again as they penetrated my being, leaving my hollow body to collapse inside itself, taking away the very life I was trying to cling to inside my mind.

"And I know it's tough," Mom continued, "thinking you have to take over, but sweetie, you need to stop this. You don't have to fill your dad's shoes, and no one is expecting you to. You'll be graduating soon and need to focus on that."

My carcass sat there, unable to move.

I didn't know if I'd heard her correctly or if my mind was so far out there that I didn't hear her at all. But now, the words I had found earlier but wasn't able to speak were forcefully ripped from my mouth. They shot across the table like arrows from a bow, screaming as they flew toward their target. "You're insane!" Finding strength, I ripped my hands from hers and slammed my fist on the table. I stood up as the words shot from my mouth, hitting any target they could find. "You are insane! You … are … *insane!*" I howled, shaking my head with each syllable, ensuring that whoever she was didn't have a chance to fight back.

My mom wept bitterly and screamed at me, over and over, to stop.

Wendy screamed at me as she ran to our mom, "Get out of here! I hate you!" Tommy also had been listening from the doorway and now added, "Why don't you just leave?"

I shoved chairs out of my way as I headed toward him in rage. "You're wrong! All of you are wrong!"

"David!" I barely heard my mom shouting. It wasn't about to stop me as I raged, full force, toward Tommy. "If you don't stop, Dr. Maiden is going to have you recommitted." She spoke strongly, getting my attention, as she tried to comfort Wendy.

I stopped short. "Recommitted? Recommitted for *what*?" I shouted, just as my cell phone rang. "*What*?" I said irritably into the phone, gripping it tightly in my hand.

"Hey, man, it's just me," Steve said, clearly surprised by the tone of my voice.

"I'll be out in a second," I said and then hung up.

As I stood there staring at my family—and they at me—I didn't know if we had anything else to say, but I had to get out of the house and away from the lies. "I'm late," I finally said. I headed outside to where Steve was waiting in his car, leaving through the garage door—and realized that my dad's car was not there. But my dad worked out of town a lot on business trips; just because his car wasn't in the garage didn't mean he hadn't been around for over a year. In fact, I had spoken with him a few days ago, and that's when he told me he would be returning from his latest trip today. And last weekend, he and I had gone to the pond and spent time fishing. My family was just playing a sick joke on me, and that was unacceptable. What was their purpose for telling me such a lie? No matter what they were saying, I would not believe them.

I got into Steve's car and shut the door hard.

"What the hell is that all about?" Steve asked.

"Nothing," I said sourly. "Let's go." I sat quietly in his car, thinking, *What did I miss that led me to this point? To the point where I feel alone and lost?*

Steve must have sensed my frustration. "You wanna tell me about it?" he finally asked.

I shook my head no; I wanted to keep my thoughts to myself. I stared out the window, not wanting to share the pain I was feeling as he drove down the street. I watched the houses become blurred as we passed them. "You know," I said calmly, "I got up this morning thinking it was Sunday. And when I asked my mom where my dad was, she told me he's been dead for over a year now." I was struggling to share my feelings and wiped at the water that formed in my eyes. The rage started growing inside of me again. "Do you believe that shit?" I shouted, becoming more frustrated and fearful at the same time. "They told me he was dead!"

Steve stopped at a red light and looked over at me in confusion. "What are you talking about?" he asked, concern in his voice.

I wondered why he didn't understand what I was saying. "When I got up this morning—"

"No, not that," Steve said. "David … you know your dad's dead. Why are you going off like this?"

My heart sank just hearing those words again. I couldn't believe this; I was hearing the same lie from one of my best friends. But I knew my dad wasn't dead, and my anger reached its boiling point and directed itself toward Steve. "You son of a bitch! How the hell can you say that?"

"Come on, man. Why are you acting this way?" Steve replied with a slight chuckle, shaking his head.

"I heard that shit this morning, and I don't want to hear it again." I felt that something else was going on that I wasn't able to figure out.

"Wow, you really were wasted last night," he said, glancing at me with disbelief.

"You know what?" I snarled. "Just let my ass out of the car."

"David, come on," Steve said. "Please just hear me out."

I decided to listen, hoping I would hear something that would help. "Okay, asshole," I said, "you seem to have all the answers. Tell me."

Steve pulled away from the traffic light as he said, "Last night we went to the bonfire because you were down."

"Down?" I interrupted.

He glanced over at me. "You really don't remember, do you?"

"Tell me," I sniped at him.

"Right ... you were down. When we got to the bonfire, you saw Rae and Jack together. And that's when the fight started."

"Wait a minute ... Jack was with Rae?" I chuckled. "Now I know you're telling me bullshit. Rae can't stand Jack—you know that." I was sure I'd caught him in a lie.

"You going to let me tell you or not?" he said, getting upset with me.

"Fine," I said, smiling.

"You saw Rae and Jack at the bonfire," Steve continued. "When you stood there looking at Rae and making comments about Jack, he came over and told you to stop calling and texting her or he'd beat the hell out of you. That's when the fight broke out. You started swinging your fists at him, but since you were too drunk and barely able to stand, he started hitting you until you fell. When you guys were on the ground, everyone started pulling you two apart. Rae got upset and told you she said to stop getting in touch with her. After that, we left to get more beer and found another party. That's where we ran into Sally and Linda, and you made a date with Sally for tonight. By the time I got you home, you were getting sick all over everything."

My mind was cloudy. "I have a date with Sally?" I asked, knowing that I didn't care for her too much.

"Yeah, we're meeting her and Linda after school today."

Now I was confused. "For your information," I told him, "I was with Rae last night. We didn't go anywhere."

"Do you even hear yourself?" Steve sniggered. "Rae's house? Jack would tear you up."

As I listened to him, it occurred to me what had happen. "Something's not right. But why didn't I notice it? How could I have missed it at the beginning?" I muttered, feeling perplexed.

"Missed what?" Steve asked. "Okay, you tell me what you think happened."

"Steve, this is a dream," I told him as I started putting the pieces together. "I didn't go out last night with you to the bonfire. I was with Rae, watching Mary. And then I went home. And the crap about Jack and me in a fight was a dream I told you the other day. Remember when we were talking at the pond, and I said I went into Jack's dream, and we fought? In his dream, he was the one drunk and making passes at Rae, not the other way around. When I confronted him in the dream, we got into a fight."

"This is a dream?" he said, laughing at me. "And you went into Jack's dream?"

"Yes, you know we have the ability to control dreams. And apparently I slipped from one dream into the next without realizing it. That's why you and everyone thinks my dad's dead." I was excited now as I understood what had transpired. "But I'm not understanding why you're not realizing we're in a dream. That hasn't happen to any of us before."

Steve laughed again and then said, "David, this isn't a dream. I don't know what you're thinking, but this is as real as it gets." He shook his head at me.

I knew he didn't believe me. "Fine. I'll show you," I said, waving my hand toward the windshield, trying to open a gateway.

"What the hell are you doing?" he asked, as he watched and heard me chant words.

"Why isn't the portal opening?" I asked very seriously—that was one of the first things Steve and I both were able to do.

"Portal? Man, you're starting to scare the shit out of me, acting this way." Now he wasn't laughing as much. "David, I don't know what you're doing, but take a look at this." He pulled down the car visor on my side, revealing a mirror.

"What the hell?" I said quietly, touching my face when I saw the cuts and black-and-blue marks on me.

"I helped your mom put you to bed last night," Steve said. "She wanted to call the cops for what Jack did, but you asked her not to."

"Let me out!" I shouted furiously. "Let my ass out of this damn car—now!"

Steve pulled over to the curb. "You got serious issues going on this morning."

I got out of his car and slammed the door as hard as I could to let him know I didn't appreciate his involvement with the joke.

As I started walking away, I could hear Steve saying something about crazy, but I wasn't able to process what he'd said about me being in a fight last night. Every detail of yesterday was very clear to me. I'd been hanging out at the pond with Rae, Bobby, and Steve until evening, and that's when I took Rae home and stayed there with her. I didn't remember being in a fight last night. But my face ... I couldn't explain the bruises and cuts.

I knew this was a dream and that explained why my family was acting strange, but I couldn't understand why Steve, who had the same capabilities as I did, didn't see this was a dream. As I continued walking, I kept trying to wake myself up and even tried to call Rae and Bobby in their dreams, but people along the sidewalk started looking at me strangely. *What's going on?* I questioned myself. I started getting worried about why I couldn't wake up.

I needed to get away and think things out. I found myself in the park at the safest place I knew—the pond. As I sat there on the bank of the pond, I started thinking of the times my dad and I would come to the park to fish and play catch. We would come here on some Saturday mornings and spend the entire day together. On Friday nights, Mom would pack a lunch for us while Dad and I put our fishing and baseball gear in the car. And we'd get up early in the morning and go to the pond. Sometimes I think we got up that early just to watch the sunrise. At midday, we'd eat the lunch Mom had made the night before and would find a note inside, telling us that she loved us. After eating, we'd get our ball and gloves out of the car and play catch on the ball diamond until one of the Little League teams came to practice or play a game. Then we would sit and watch the players until suppertime and then head back home. We didn't do it every Saturday, but when we did, we enjoyed the time we shared.

I tried numerous times throughout the day to call Dad on his cell phone. Each time I called, the person on the other end told me I had the wrong number, that he'd had the phone number—my Dad's cell phone number—for almost a year, and if I didn't stop calling, he would notify the police. I still refused to believe my dad was dead; I believed this was just a dream. But the longer I sat there thinking about what was going on, the more I thought maybe Mom was right.

Maybe I did have a delusional disorder and couldn't accept the fact my dad was dead. And because I couldn't handle it, I'd created this dream world. But if I did have mental issues, why didn't I remember any of it? Why was everything around me normal, except for certain aspects of my life? As evening came and the night sky took over, I left for home, walking in a light snowfall that reminded me spring had only started. I wished for all of this to go away.

I found my mom asleep on the couch when I got home. She'd probably cried herself to sleep since I hadn't answered the phone when she'd called me numerous times. I didn't wake her; I went into the garage to verify that my dad's car still wasn't there. Mom was awake when I returned to the living room. I sat down on the chair, feeling sad, lonely, and frightened.

She looked at me with sorrow and said in a loving, caring voice, "It's late. Maybe you should get some sleep." I stared at her, looking for some kind of answers. When I didn't respond, she changed the subject. "I know it's hard for you, breaking up with Rae, especially after going through what you've been through this last year."

"Rae? I've been trying to get a hold of her, but she won't answer," I said sadly.

"After last night, you might want to stay away from her," she advised, reminding me of the fight I couldn't remember.

I couldn't understand how my world got turned upside down. I finally broke down, pleading for help. "Mom, what's going on with me?"

She didn't answer me; instead, she got up from the couch and kissed my head. Then she handed me a newspaper clipping and a pill container, giving me time to figure things out. After watching her disappear down the hall to her room, I glanced down at the pill container—the prescription label had my name on it. But even worse was the clipping. It read "Andrew M. Birch, passed away ..." I sat in the living room, feeling abandoned and helpless, as I read my dad's obituary.

What I'd thought was a dream actually was real, just as my family and Steve had told me.

When I awoke the next morning, I didn't feel as lively as I had the day before after having a dream about Rae. I lay in bed, wishing I had woken from this nightmare. But seeing the obituary on the nightstand, I had to accept what had been handed to me. I thought about staying home from school, but Mom started banging on the door.

"Come on, David. You're going to be late," she called from the other side of the door.

I looked at the obituary and felt nauseated. "I'm staying home!" I shouted.

Mom came into my room and sat on the bed. Her face still had the compassionate look it'd had last night. She spoke softly to me. "In order to get past this, you need to move forward."

"Here," I said, handing her the newspaper clipping.

She took the article from my hand and glanced down at it. "Honey, you only have a few months until graduation." She stood up, tugging on my foot. "Besides, you've gotten past these episodes before. You'll get through this one," she said, and then she left me alone with my thoughts.

After showering, I called Rae again but got her voicemail. I checked my phone history for the last time she had called or texted me. *Two months ago?* Her last text said we were through and not to contact her again.

"Come on; it's getting late," Mom said, interrupting my thoughts as she opened the door.

"I'm coming," I responded. I held my towel tightly around me as I walked over and shut the door.

It wasn't that I was trying to be rude or mean to my mother; it's just I didn't want anyone around while I was trying to think.

And being alone at that moment was what I wanted the most. Eventually, I headed downstairs and went into the kitchen. My mom, Tommy, and Wendy were sitting at the kitchen table, eating and not saying a word. I joined them; Mom already had my plate on the table.

As we ate in silence, Tommy and Wendy kept glancing over at me. I still felt I needed questions answered, but I didn't want to start another argument. Finally, I had to ask because I hoped she would tell me everything was okay. "Mom, what are we going to do?"

She looked up from her plate. "In what way, sweetie?"

"I don't know, but after yesterday ... after what I said ... I wasn't sure how you would be feeling this morning."

She looked at me but took a moment to think of her words. When she spoke, her voice seemed serene. "We need to let yesterday go and concentrate on making today and tomorrow better. I know it hurts, and it does take time to heal. You've gone through a lot this year, but believe me, things will work out."

At school I walked around in a daze from class to class, trying to remain coherent in my new world. It seemed to be moving in slow motion when I passed other kids, all of whom appeared to be gazing back at me. I watched their lips move but was unable to hear their voices. I assumed they were talking about the bruises on my face.

Where once I had friends around me as I walked these halls, now I had emptiness on my left and my right as I continued down the corridors, watching the line of students passing me. I saw Rae coming my direction, and my heart started pounding harder. I tried to slow my breathing down—I wanted to talk with her. My slow-motion actions caught up with the rest of the kids, and I began hearing their voices get louder as I got closer to her.

She made brief eye contact with me and then quickly turned down another passageway, disappearing in the crowd of students somewhere in the cafeteria. When I got there, I sat down to eat alone.

Steve came up to the lunch table with a tray in hand. "You still pissed at me?" he asked. When I didn't answer, he raised his voice and said, "Hello? You still mad at me?"

Finally, I shook my head. "No, I'm not pissed," I told him as he sat down across from me.

He noticed that I was staring at Rae, who was sitting a few tables across from us. "You've got to let her go," he said.

"I don't even know how we broke up. It's a blur to me," I said, confused and unable to look away from her. "Regardless, you might just want to stop staring." Steve nodded his head toward Jack, who was just passing our table and heading toward Rae.

"Maybe your body is just fighting the medicine."

"I guess," I replied and then went back to my staring.

"Didn't the doctor increase it a few months back?" he asked, as if I should have known.

I gazed at him, thinking about what he'd just said. "I don't know," I replied.

He took a bite of his lunch. "Why are you looking at me like that?" he asked.

Once again I started feeling as if something was wrong. Where I was feeling lost, Steve gave the impression that he knew everything that was going on. "How do you know that my medicine was increased?" I asked.

"Come on. What's the deal?" he said defensively.

"I'm serious. You seem to have all the answers lately. How do you know that my medicine was increased?" I was thinking he had an ulterior motive.

Steve looked at me sternly. "I do have all the answers," he said boldly.

"What?" I replied, chuckling at him.

"We've been friends for a long time. I was there when your dad passed away, when you were committed in the hospital after you lost it, and yes, I was there when you and Rae broke up," Steve said, without blinking his eyes. "The point is, I know you have a disorder. And it will take time. Until then, we do what we have to do." He stopped speaking, letting me soak up what he just said.

"But that's just it," I said seriously. "I don't remember my dad passing away. I don't remember being in the hospital. And damn it, God knows I don't know why Rae and I broke up." I felt sickened by my lack of understanding.

And then he tried to lighten the mood, saying, "And don't act like I'm your new girlfriend just because I know this much about you."

But my mood couldn't be lifted. I needed to know the truth—truth that I felt was being hidden from me. I did smile a little at Steve's comment, though, and then felt like an ass for questioning what I saw as a motive.

"I'm sorry," I said. "Maybe you're right. Maybe it is the medicine." I glanced around the cafeteria. "I'm just feeling strange. I feel as if someone is watching me." Steve didn't respond, so I continued. "And you want to know what's even stranger? Once in a while, I hear a faint voice inside my head, calling to me. And the voice I'm hearing ... is Rae's."

Steve didn't have any more answers for me. We finished eating lunch in silence, just giving each other a look now and then. I could tell Steve was feeling sorry for me, as he looked at me sympathetically. But what could he really do or say? I had to figure this out.

Finally, seeing me look over at Rae and Jack again, he said, "So, with all that said, what's your plan later today, other than trying to stare Jack down? You want to hang out with Sally, Linda, and me since we didn't get together last night?"

"I'm not sure," I said. "Bobby and I were supposed to meet

up later tonight. But I haven't seen or heard from him in a couple of days. And his phone is not in service. I figure I'll drive over to his grandma's and see if he's there. You haven't seen him, have you?" I hoped Steve might know where my other friend was.

Steve shook his head, seeming confused. "Who?"

"Bobby. Have you seen him lately?" I responded, getting irritated that he looked puzzled. "Bobby Eriks. Our friend," I told him.

"David, we don't have a friend named Bobby Eriks." Steve said flatly as he stood up from the table. "At least, I don't." He walked away, leaving me to sit there in shock. Why had Steve said that?

It was at the beginning of our sixth-grade year when Bobby and his parents moved into the subdivision across the street from mine, but it was during spring break when we really got to know each other. Warm days were melting the snow and ice, and I couldn't wait to go fishing in my favorite spot at the pond. Waking up early and grabbing a fishing pole, I'd ride my bike to the park, only to find Bobby sitting on his tackle box, eating a sandwich, with his fishing line already in the water.

The first time it happened, I jumped off my bike and let him know that was my spot. We soon found ourselves rolling on the ground, fighting over that piece of the pond. We hit, kicked, and called each other names, but Bobby suddenly shouted, "My pole!" He stopped fighting and ran over to the bank, reaching his pole in time to keep it from going into the water.

I was no longer concerned about saving my spot. I ran over to him and shouted, "Reel it in!" He stumbled over his gear, and I kicked it out of the way as fast as I could. He fought with the fish—and then his pole broke in two. As he kept reeling in, I held up the end of the pole, helping him to keep it steady.

We finally saw the fish jump out of the water and land closer to shore. Once we finally got the fish on land, we stood there grinning at each other as we wiped the blood and sweat from ourselves.

Since that day of fighting and fishing, we've been best of friends.

Sometimes when Bobby would spend the night, we'd sneak out of the house with our poles and a lantern to go fishing until just before daylight. Then we would race back home before anyone knew we were out. One night my dad caught us sneaking into the house carrying fish. Instead of telling Mom, my dad helped us clean the fish before Mom knew what we had done.

Steve's response to my question shocked me. He—along with my family—had me believing that my dad was dead, that Rae and I had broken up, and now, that my one of best friends didn't even exist! I no longer felt sorry for myself; my anger overflowed.

"You bastard!" I called after him, trying to get his attention before he got too far away from me. "How dare you say that and just leave?" I stormed after him.

"David, it's just your delusion," he replied unsympathetically.

"I may have issues with my dad and Rae," I said loudly, "but don't tell me Bobby doesn't exist." To stress my point, I tossed my lunch tray at his feet.

Steve didn't say anything; he just looked around at the other kids in the lunchroom and started to walk away again.

"Why the hell are you doing this?" I now questioned his sincerity in our friendship.

"You're mentally ill," he said coldly. "Have you taken your medicine today?"

"The hell with you," I growled and then hit him in the face with my fist, sending him to the ground. I was standing over

Steve, waiting for him to get up, when I heard one of the teachers shout, "Mr. Birch!"

The voice came again, louder and harsher. "Mr. Birch!" And then I felt him grab my arm.

"Leave me alone!" I roared, trying to pull away from him.

"Get the security guard," the teacher instructed a student who stood nearby.

Still struggling to get free, I picked up a chair and started swinging it until the teacher finally let me go. The security guard came rushing into the cafeteria, and I threw the chair toward him. It smashed into an empty table as he moved out of the way and called for help on his radio. Jack and other kids started heading toward me, but I took off running, out the doors that led outside and then to the school parking lot, where my car was parked.

I realized, though, that the security guards—the first one had gotten reinforcements—were close behind me, and I'd never reach my car before they caught me. So I ran to the underground walkway that separated the old high school from the new one, and then made my way through yards and backstreets until I stood on the train tracks to catch my breath and looked back to be sure I had lost them.

From there I walked to the park and stayed in the woods until evening, when parents brought the kids for ball practice. I didn't see the police or anyone else who might be looking for me, so I walked to the bleachers, trying to blend in with others who were watching the team practice. Although I felt safe in the small crowd on the bleachers, I still got the feeling that someone was watching me. I looked nervously around the park.

As I listened to and watched the kids play around me, I wondered how I had lost my world in two days. Yesterday seemed so clear to me when I woke up, but others had no memory of my world, and they continued to pull me deeper into the nightmare.

And today, in their world, I had no recollection of the events they told me had taken place. *What is the answer I need to figure this out?* I thought.

The coach was barking out instructions, but the train in the background of the ball diamond soon drowned out his voice—and it brought me back from my thoughts. I was starting to feel insecure and worried, so I walked back over to the pond, talking to myself, wondering how I came to be here. As I got closer to the pond's pier, I saw a girl walking toward me. "You sure are hard to get a hold of," she said sweetly. "We've been searching for you."

"Mary?" I wondered if it was truly Rae's little sister standing in front of me or just another delusion I was having.

"Yes, David, it's me," she replied, smiling with joy.

"What are you doing here?" I asked, looking puzzled. I didn't know why she would be coming from the woods.

She reached out to take my hand. "Let's go home," she said, trying to lead me.

I planted my feet and wouldn't follow. "Mary, what's going on?" I asked, as I looked around for others.

"Okay, I tried it your way," she said with a laugh. "Now, I'm gonna do it my way." She smiled a girlish smile—and then I blacked out.

CHAPTER 2 DREAM CONTROL

I was lying on the sands of the beach, watching the night sky light up with shooting stars that traveled the universe, disappearing somewhere beyond the horizon of the sea. As I became engulfed from her gaze, I reached out to caress her beautiful face. I was captivated by the moon's reflection in her eyes. It invited me to embrace her warmth, which covered our passion like a blanket, while the cool breeze drifting off the ocean encompassed us.

Our souls quickly became entangled, just as a rose vine wrapped around itself, ultimately bringing forth the radiance of a rose. I could feel our heartbeats pounding hard and fast as the waves rushed across the sand, drowning out the world around us. With the heat of her lips on mine, we gasped for life as our breath merged into one and our bodies quivered.

I gently kissed her neck, and reaching down, stroking her thighs, I could feel the chill bumps rise under her clothes. Not wanting to let her go, I soon found my hands holding her waist as my lips passed over her belly, barely touching her soft skin with each kiss. I wanted to let her know how I felt. "Rae, I lo—"

Shit, I spoke softly to myself as I opened my eyes to the bedroom ceiling above me. I'd been awakened from my dream by my mother's voice, which was still ringing in my ears. "David, I said *now*!"

I pulled the covers over my head, wishing I could return to my fantasy of Rae.

It was Friday morning—another week had come and gone, and as far as I was concerned, it was one more day closer to graduation. There were only a few more months, and I was like any other graduating senior; I was counting down the days to saying good-bye to teachers and homework but most important, good-bye to the words "time to get up for school." I wasn't against learning; I just felt I had better things to do with my life, and I was eager to get started.

My mom shouted again for us to hurry. I kicked off the covers and decided to skip my shower. I threw on some clothes that were lying on the floor and went downstairs.

"Aren't you going to eat?" she questioned me, as I was about to leave.

"No," I snapped. I still felt irritated about her interrupting my dream. I shut the door behind me and was heading for my car when I saw Jack driving down the street.

I didn't want to talk with him, so I quickly got in and shut the car door, but he honked, trying to get my attention, as he pulled up next to me. Although Jack lived a few houses away from me, we never got along. He was not only a conceited jock and was condescending, but he treated people as if they were second-class citizens. However, that wasn't my main issue with Jack.

Jack still had feelings for Rae, and whenever he could, he'd put obstacles in the way of our relationship, trying to break us up. Rae and Jack had dated since junior high until the summer after our sophomore year in high school, when she caught him making out with Carmen, one of her best friends, when he was supposed to be on a date with Rae. It took time to get over the hurt, but when she did, Rae and I got together and have been together for a year now.

I rolled down the window and called out without looking at him, "What do you want, Jack?"

"When are you going to get into modern times?" He sneered at the dents and rust on my car.

"If that's all you want, I need to go," I snapped at him, becoming more annoyed.

Oblivious to what I just said, he said, "What do you think?" He then revved up his new car that his parents had given him as an early graduation present.

I rolled my eyes again and shook my head and told him I had to go.

"Hey, I'm just wondering if you're going to the bonfire tonight," he said, sounding as if he truly was interested.

I looked at him through narrowed eyes. "Why does it matter what I'm doing?" I asked suspiciously.

He smiled again. "Jill is going to be there, and I heard she was looking for you."

I thought he was just trying to put another hurdle between Rae and me. "Why should I care if she's there?" I asked, sighing.

Jack shrugged. "I just wanted to let you know in case you weren't doing anything with Rae tonight." He spoke as if he was sincerely looking out for my best interest.

"If you must know," I said, feeling pleased with myself, "Rae and I are celebrating our one-year anniversary. What do you think about that? A whole year we've been dating." I smiled back at him, believing I got the better of the conversation.

It was a shame he didn't stay around long enough to find out what I got her. Hell, I thought we were starting to have a civilized talk for once. But I guess not since he squealed his tires as he sped away, running the stop sign just ahead. *Jackass*, I thought when he almost crashed into another car. We'd given him the nickname "Jackass"—at least behind his back—because he was the biggest ass around. And I knew he wasn't concerned with anyone's welfare, let alone mine, so I'm pretty sure he didn't tell me about Jill for my benefit.

Jill was my first love in freshmen year. We did everything together, until she broke my heart by telling me we were just too good of friends to be dating. When our relationship came to an end, it left a scar, and Jack wanted to remind me of it. Just as Jill was my first love, Rae was Jack's. But I've learned that another love will always replace the first love; that's why it was called "first" love.

As I reached Steve's house, I could tell by the expression on his face that he was upset that I was late.

"Where have you been?" he demanded as he got in the car.

"Don't ask," I replied, irritated with how my morning had gone. My cell phone rang as I started to drive away. "Now what?" I sighed. It was Bobby, wondering where we were.

"You seem pissed," Steve observed. "What happened? Your mom wake you up again from a dream about Rae?" He chuckled at me.

"It's not only that. Tonight's our anniversary, and I didn't have enough money to get Rae the ring I wanted to," I responded in disappointment.

"I have a five on me," Steve said, reaching for his wallet.

"Great," I said, "that leaves me about two hundred short."

Steve put away his wallet without giving me the five. "Yep, you're screwed," he said unsympathetically and laughed.

As we approached Bobby's house, I saw him in the middle of the street, waving us down. "I wouldn't have expected him to be in a hurry," I said.

"What excuse are we using today for being late? I still have plenty more," he said, smiling as he climbed into the backseat.

Steve told Bobby that my mom interrupted another dream, and Bobby joined in the fun of my bad luck. "What about the bonfire? Are we going? There's a private party afterward," Bobby said as he slapped Steve and me on the shoulders.

"I can't. I'm hanging with Rae tonight," I told him. My mood began changing as I thought about spending the evening with her.

"That's right. I say let's go and rub it in Jackass's face," Bobby said, grinning as he remembered how Rae and I first got together. Although it was sounding very tempting, I let Bobby know I was sure Rae wouldn't go for it.

"Well, look at that," Bobby said, after we pulled into the school's parking lot.

"He's a jerk," I responded. Jack was standing next to Rae's car, not letting her out. Apparently, the only way he could get a captive audience was to stand next to someone's car door and not let him or her out until he got done flapping his lips about nothing.

"And the other asses are with him," Steve remarked about Jack's friends.

"Well, let's go rescue your princess from the dragon," Bobby said, smiling as if he was ready for a confrontation.

"I see you finally made it!" Jack shouted at me as I headed toward Rae. "I was betting you wouldn't make it in that piece of shit." He started laughing with his friends. Rolling my eyes and not saying a word, I walked over and stood between him and Rae's car.

"This way, my beautiful princess," I said, smiling at Rae.

She gave me an odd look but said, "Why thank you, my prince."

Steve and Bobby started laughing when Jack went back to his followers.

"My princess?" she said, questioning my choice of words.

"I figured the dragon was trying to devour you. So naturally I had to rescue you," I told her and winked.

"Check that out," Bobby said as we headed toward the school building.

"Lillie is never going to notice you," Steve told Bobby as he shoved him a little.

Seeing other guys around Lillie, Bobby shook his head and said, "With all those dogs swarming around her like bees in a honey hive, I'll never get to taste the sweet nectar she has blossoming inside her."

"That's just not right," Rae said to Bobby.

"You got your man," Bobby said as he slapped my hand in the air. "I just want to make sure she finds her right man. Me!" Bobby looked at the smirk on Steve's face. "And what are you smiling about?"

"Maybe she would want me," Steve suggested.

"Want you? She's not going to be interested in you," Bobby said, looking at Steve peculiarly.

"I think she would rather be with me," Rae said, chuckling.

"Girl, you're sick," Bobby commented, without laughing this time.

"Oh, don't be that way," Rae told him as she put her arm around him. "I might even consider dating you."

We started laughing as we headed inside the school building before the last bell rang.

After telling Bobby to meet me at my car after lunch, I walked Rae to her first class, giving her a kiss and hug good-bye, and then headed to my class to start one more day closer to the last. One thing I loved about being a senior was a day like today, where the sun was shining, melting what little snow there was left on the ground, and having a half-day in school.

Walking in the cafeteria at lunchtime, I found Rae sitting with Sally, her best friend. Just as I sat down with my lunch tray across from Rae, Sally started in on me.

"You know, you get to see her all the time. Don't you have a half-day? And why can't she and I just hang out without you?" Sally said, sounding upset and not taking a breath between each question.

"I like you, too, Sally," I replied with a smile, not giving her the satisfaction of having the upper hand. I didn't hate Sally, but

I didn't care for her much either. She was right about one thing, though—we both wanted to be with Rae, and we seemed to be in competition with one another.

Even though I dreaded talking to her at times, I asked in a fake worried voice why she didn't like me. Knowing I didn't care either way, she responded with a false smile and proceeded to talk to Rae as if I wasn't there. Motor mouth. That's what she reminded me of, because she wouldn't take a breath to let anyone else say a word. But as I sat there eating my lunch, biding my time, I heard, "Oh, wait. I want to show you something," and she started looking in her purse.

That was the break I needed. "Where are we going to go celebrate tonight?" I quickly asked Rae the question before Sally's engine started up again. You could have almost put me in the ground when Sally got done staring through me with her spiteful look. The chill that ran down my spine wasn't because I was concerned about Sally, but it reminded me why I enjoyed pissing her off so much when I could.

Finally, regaining her self-control, Sally continued looking at me as she pulled a twenty-dollar bill from her purse instead of the necklace she was going to show Rae. "I'm amazed you even remembered," she told me and handed the money to Rae.

"You bet against me?" I questioned, although I laughed as I enjoyed Sally's loss. Without saying a word, she twitched her nose and left the table, leaving Rae and me alone.

"You've got to stop picking on her," Rae said with a smile of her own. "And I can't go out tonight. I have to watch Mary while my dad goes bowling."

"More likely the bar," I responded without thinking.

"That's not fair, David," she replied in a hurt voice.

"Look, I'm sorry. But he's been like that for a few years now, always leaving you home to watch Mary while he goes out drinking." I knew the apology wasn't coming out right. Getting more upset, she said she was done with lunch and left the table, leaving me there thinking of the stupid words I'd spoken, especially on our anniversary. Rae was the one who'd been taking care of Mary for the last few years after her mother passed away. And I guess that's why I didn't care too much for Mr. Woods. I felt he was always putting his responsibilities on Rae.

I caught up with Rae in the hall, right before she was going into her next class. "Rae, I really am sorry," I said softly, hoping she wouldn't stay mad at me.

"I know you didn't mean it. It's just ... I've been thinking about my mom and her not being here for my graduation." There was sorrow in her voice as she wiped a tear from her cheek.

Wow, sometimes I really put my foot in my mouth—I guess we all do, and we may not realize how bad we did until we're standing there feeling as if we just destroyed someone's dream.

Rae gave me a hug and kissed me to let me know that she knew I wasn't trying to hurt her; then she went into the classroom.

"So where to?" Bobby asked when I got to the car.

"I don't care," I said, tossing him the keys to drive anywhere. He sensed something was on my mind, so he drove to the pond, where we spent a lot of time thinking or just hanging out. It was a place we could relax and enjoy talking without disturbance from other people, especially with it still being cold outside.

"Remember how we used to come here and fish?" I reminisced.

"Yeah, I do," Bobby answered. We both started chuckling as we enjoyed thinking of the past. Then Bobby changed our conversation from the past to our future. "What are your plans after graduation?" he asked.

I wasn't sure what I wanted to do. I'd thought about different careers, but I couldn't stick with only one path as I thought about my future.

My dad wanted me to follow in his footsteps and work as a financial consultant, but that didn't appeal to me, especially when I'd rather spend the money instead of investing it. Besides, his position took him out of town a lot. So I could only tell Bobby, "I don't know. I don't have the grades to get into college, other than state. You?"

"Man, I want more adventure in my life. I was thinking about heading to California and finding a DJ job," he said with enthusiasm as he thought about his dream. He had his own setup at home, and when his grandmother was visiting Bobby's mom and dad, who had moved to California, leaving Bobby with his grandma to finish school, he would have parties so he could practice being a DJ.

"Oh, shit!" I said as my cell phone rang. Bobby and I had sat at the pond all afternoon, talking about many things; I had forgotten Steve needed a ride home. "We're on our way," I said into the phone and quickly hung up. And then I noticed Rae had sent a text, telling me she was heading home and to call her later. After picking Steve up from school, we left for home.

"Are you going to pick me up when you go to the bonfire?" Steve asked Bobby, knowing I wasn't going and Bobby didn't have a date.

"You need your own damn car," Bobby said. "What if I find a lady? You think I want you taking her seat?"

"Who do you think is going to be sitting in the seat? Lillie?" Steve said, laughing.

"What about you?" Bobby asked me. "Are you going to Rae's?"

"Once I drop off you and Steve, I'm calling Rae to find out if she wants me to come over."

I pulled into Bobby's driveway.

"Yeah, I'll take your skinny ass to the bonfire," Bobby told Steve. "But if I get hooked up, your ass is gonna walk home." He laughed as he walked away from the car.

Steve and I rode in silence until we reached his house. Then, as we pulled into his driveway, Steve asked, "Are you still planning on taking me to my sister's tomorrow?"

"Bobby's right; you need your own damn car," I said, chuckling.

"Come on. My foster parents aren't going to buy me one, and my sister only lives a short distance from here. And you know as well as I do, working at Burger and Drink isn't going to buy me a car."

I let him worry for just a moment and then said, "Yeah, I'll drop you off."

Steve was a year younger than Bobby and I. His parents had given him up for adoption when he was born, and his adoptive parents abandoned him when he was two years old. He'd been raised in foster homes since then. He moved in with his current foster parents about three years ago, and that's how we met him—we'd seen him alone at movies, eating lunch by himself, and getting picked on at school. You might say Bobby and I kind of adopted Steve, in our own way.

Although Sue wasn't his biological sister, they treated each other as if they were siblings from the start. She was about four years older than Steve, and they'd met some years ago, living with the same foster family, where they got to know each other pretty well. She was now living on her own with a toddler close by, and Steve would go over every few weeks to visit and help with the baby, since the dad was nowhere to be found.

"Your mom wants to know if you're going to dinner and a movie with us," my dad asked when I came into the house.

"No, I'm hoping to go to Rae's," I replied, starting to head upstairs.

"She can come with us," Mom said as she came into the living room.

"She's watching Mary. And besides, it's our first anniversary. So we're just gonna hang out and watch movies," I said, although I hoped that wasn't what we were really going to do.

"Movies, huh?" Dad chuckled, putting on his jacket.

"Alex, stop," Mom said, smiling at him.

"Well, you and I both know what watching movies, home alone, was like when we were that age," he said, slapping her rear. "Let's go, Tommy and Wendy!" Mom shouted up the stairs. She turned to me.

"How late are you going to be?"

"I don't know; maybe I'll spend the night," I replied and winked at my dad.

"Come on, everyone, our reservation's at 5:30. And you," my dad told me as he was walking out the door, "you don't be out too late. We have yard work tomorrow."

"It's Saturday, and I don't have to go into work. Can't we do it Sunday?" I asked, but he was already shutting the door and didn't hear me.

I called Rae as soon as my family left. "You still mad at me for what I said?" I asked, feeling a little worried she might be.

"No, I'm not mad," she replied. Her tone of voice sounded happier.

"Since we can't go out, you want me to come over and help babysit?"

I could hear Mary's voice in the background, shouting, "I'm not a baby!"

"Get away from my door, brat!" Rae shouted and then took her cell phone off the speaker. "Now!" she said one more time, knowing Mary was still on the other side of the door. Rae waited a few seconds and then opened her bedroom door to ensure Mary wasn't listening to our conversation. "Be here around 7:30," Rae said.

"Okay, I'll take a shower and be there," I told her, feeling excited about spending time with her.

"I hope so. I could smell you at lunch." She chuckled and hung up the phone.

I had extra time after my shower before I needed to head to Rae's, so I turned on the TV and watched until I heard a car start up outside. I got up and looked out the window and shouted, "Hey! That's my car!" I ran out the door, shouting at the thief to stop. I wasn't able to catch up to the car as it ran the stop sign and turned down the street. I started running through yards and climbing fences, trying to catch up to my car before it left the subdivision. As I ran into the middle of the main road, I shouted, "Stop!" and held my hands out in front of me, as a pickup truck was about to hit me.

I tripped and fell to the ground, trying to catch my breath and feeling my heart pound as sweat poured from my body. I was astonished that the truck was no longer moving.

I got up and walked over to the door. The driver and passenger were sitting there, smiling, looking straight ahead as if nothing had happened.

"Hey," I said, poking the driver's shoulder. "Hey, asshole," I spoke again, feeling my legs give way when he didn't respond. I stood there, holding onto the truck, and thought, *Where the hell am I?*

I didn't see any movement from other cars on the road, although there were drivers inside. A little girl who was playing jump rope was frozen in mid-air as she made another jump, while her two friends stood immobile, smiling as they watched her. As I continued looking in amazement, I noticed it wasn't only the people who weren't moving. Birds in the air were now as dots in the sky or in mid-flight as if they were about to land in trees. It gave me a creepy feeling. *Is this a dream?* I asked myself.

And then, I noticed my own car was down the road, also stopped in the middle of the street as the driver was turning a corner. I ran toward it, shouting, "That's my car!" Just as I reached it, my car started dissolving from view. "This is a dream," I said when my car completely vanished. A phone was ringing somewhere. As I looked around to find where the ringing was coming from, everything else started fading, leaving me staring at the TV as I sat in the chair.

Trying to get my bearings, I grabbed the phone and heard Rae's voice on the other end.

"Where are you?" Rae asked.

"What?" I said. I got up from the chair to look out the window to see if my car was still there.

"David, it's 8:00. You were supposed to be here thirty minutes ago." I could hear the concern in her voice.

"I'm sorry; I'm leaving now," I said.

"What happened?"

"I'll explain when I get there," I replied and then hung up the phone.

When I got to Rae's house, we sat on the couch, and I told her I had fallen asleep watching TV and had a dream. I described the dream and the eerie feeling I had, seeing everything frozen. "And after I said, 'It's a dream,' everything faded," I explained.

"You had a lucid dream," she informed me.

"Lucid dream?"

"You're getting ready to graduate from high school and you don't know about lucid dreams?" she said with a smirk. "Lucid dreams are when you're aware that you're dreaming when you're in a dream."

"But I wasn't aware I was dreaming," I interrupted.

"No? You said you told yourself it was a dream, and that's when things started to fade," she reminded me.

We finished talking about the dream, and then I handed her the ring I'd gotten for her. "It wasn't the one I really wanted to get you."

"I like it," she said, smiling as she put it on and then gave me a kiss.

We had an enjoyable evening, sitting there on the couch, cuddling, and talking about the last year we'd spent together. Mary came downstairs and saw Rae and me kissing. "That's gross!" she said.

"Well, I guess it's time for me to go," I told Rae, losing the romantic mood I was having; plus, it was getting late.

When I got home from Rae's house, my mom was waiting for me. "Did you have a nice time with Rae?" she asked.

I smiled, thinking about all that we did. "Yes," I answered.

"Well?" Dad said as he handed my mom a drink.

"What?" I tried to figure out what he was referring to.

After shaking his head back and forth, he finally said, "The ring?"

"Yes, I gave it to her," I said and then went upstairs.

As I lay on the bed, thinking about the dream I'd had earlier and what Rae had told me about lucid dreams, I became a little obsessed with the notion of dreams. I wanted to find out more about lucid dreams, but now, another thought consumed me: if I'm aware of my dreams, can I control them? I got on the computer and started researching lucid dreams. That's when I came across a Web page that read "How to Lucid Dream."

After arming myself with information from the Web site, I went to sleep ... only to wake up at Burger and Drink fast food, where Jack was coming through the door. I saw one of my co-workers take Jack's order. As I started to smile at him, Jack said, "What's your problem?" I grinned harder—he was standing in front of the counter, wearing only his boxers.

"I'm dreaming," I said, as I heard everyone laughing. And then, as everything started vanishing from view, I tried to keep myself from waking up by shouting, "Not yet!"

Jack, clearly embarrassed, started to run out the door, and I realized the dream was staying stable—and that's when I found myself being conscious of the dream itself.

"Hey, Jackass," I called to him as he was about to go out the door.

He looked back at me. "What do you want?"

I thought about floating, and as I did, I rose up a little and headed toward Jack … and then, my eyes opened as I rolled over and looked at the desk in my room.

I was excited about having controlled some aspects of the dream but disappointed I had woken up. Unable to go back to sleep, I did more research on lucid dreams until I had to pick up Steve. I explained to him what had happened in my dream as I drove him to his sister's house.

"I don't remember my dreams," he said quietly.

"Is something bothering you?" I asked. When he didn't respond, I asked how the bonfire had gone last night, and that's when he told me that he'd been beaten up. Apparently, after Bobby had dropped him off at home. Steve was a little too drunk to go inside the house right away, so, not wanting to get into trouble with his foster parents, he went for a walk around the neighborhood—and that's where he ran into John Stier.

John was a bully and someone who had picked on Steve for a long time. For the most part, as long as Bobby or I was around, John didn't bother Steve. Bobby was built bigger than John and was more than happy to challenge him. Steve, however, being a small person and somewhat nerdy, wasn't able to defend himself against John, who seemed twice Steve's size.

Last night, John had started picking on Steve, telling him he had no business going to the bonfire. When Steve tried to walk away, John tripped him and kicked him in the gut as he lay on the sidewalk.

"Don't you do anything, Steve," I said. "Bobby and I will go after John."

Steve shook his head and said, "No. Let it go."

I dropped Steve off at Sue's and went home to help my dad

clean the yard.

I was exhausted after helping my dad. I took a shower and then climbed in bed and fell asleep. I was standing next to a lake and saw how the clouds changed colors from pink, to red, to a dark blue, and then back to pink again. Seagulls were flying and landing on the sandy shore of the lake. "Hey, take the line!" I heard someone shout from the sailboat as it began tossing in the waves that now looked like the ocean.

Men and women on the boat were eating lunch at a picnic table. As the waves came over the edge of the boat, a man in shorts tossed the rope to me. As soon as I touched the rope, I was immediately taken aboard. The boat now was a yacht, and I stared at individuals who wore winter clothes and others who barely wore anything as they lay on deck chairs in the sun. As the feeling came upon me that I was having a dream, I wondered if I could manipulate the dream.

I wished the people in winter coats were gone, and they started disappearing as I looked at each one. I waved my hand in the direction of the water, and then we were all standing on large boulders in the middle of a river. *Well, that didn't work out very well*, I thought. Trying again, I waved my hand and thought about being on shore.

Opening my eyes, the people were no longer there, but I was standing in the middle of an empty lot, listening to noise from the surrounding buildings. I was unable to control what I was doing. I was floating above the ground, drifting along as the breeze took me. I saw people vanish and reappear quickly, and I felt the urge to get out of there—but I wasn't sure where "there" was. After telling myself I needed to wake up, I once again stared at my bedroom ceiling.

Although I wasn't able to direct the dream as I wanted, I was very excited to know that when I tried, different scenes of the dream changed, and not only that, I was able to control some things, such as floating above the ground and when I wanted the scenery to change. Over the next week or so when I dreamed, I would look for particulars within the dream to confirm that I was actually dreaming.

As my fascination with dreams grew more intense. I started paying attention to what was happening in them. That is, when I dreamed, sometimes I knew the people in them, but most of the time I didn't. They would come and go and not even be concerned that I watched or changed the dream on them. So I wondered if I could influence the people in my dreams as I did the surroundings.

"Excuse me, sir," I asked the man, who looked to be in his thirties, standing on the sidewalk.

"Yes?" he said.

"Can I have some money?"

"I don't have any," he responded and walked away.

I felt disappointed the dream didn't go as I'd wanted it to, but I had to try again. This time, I wouldn't ask; I would tell someone to do what I wanted him or her to do.

Men and women with tattoos on their oversized arms stood next to their bikes drinking beer and listening to loud music at the corner bar. I wasn't sure I wanted to approach them, but I slowly walked up to them. Even though I knew this was a dream, I still was worried about what could happen. "Turn that damn music down," I said with a cracking voice.

I was shaking inside of myself and feeling sweaty. I kept telling myself this was a dream and nothing more, and then a huge, shirtless guy with tattoos all over him started walking in my direction. He brushed his long hair out of his face and looked down at me, towering over me.

"I said turn that shit down!" I shouted. My words seemed to fall on deaf ears, as he took another step my way and rested his chest on my face.

This isn't working, I thought. As deeply as I could, I bellowed, "Now!" I felt a force come out from me and spread outward, and that giant of a man turned around, walked back to the bar, talked to someone who stood in the doorway, and soon, the music was turned off. The man looked back toward me, and I waved my hand just as I opened my eyes. Sweat rolled off my forehead as I looked at the ceiling once again, still trying to catch my breath.

Lying there in the darkness of my room, I wondered if it was just luck that the beast at the bar had someone turn the music off. Was it because of my ability to control him, or had he wanted to give a kid a break? Having plenty of time before daylight was upon me, I wanted desperately to find out if it was luck or not. Suddenly, I appeared in another dream and saw people vanishing and reappearing.

Making my way through the park, I saw people laughing, playing sports, and enjoying time outside. I came across two individuals who were a little larger than me but about the same size and as muscular as Bobby. "Move your ass," one of the men said as I watched women playing volleyball—I was blocking his view of the women. Not saying a word but thinking what I wanted him to do, I waved my hand in front of his face, and he suddenly punched the other guy. As the other guy stood up and was ready to hit him back, I said, "Don't do it," in a stern voice.

I started laughing, and the second man spoke to me in anger as he wiped the blood from his mouth. "And why are you laughing?"

I didn't like the way he'd talked to me, and because I believed I could make him do what I wanted him to do, I told him, "I want you to go running through the women's volleyball game naked." I started laughing out loud as he did exactly as I said. I clapped my hands together and opened my eyes in reality.

I started feeling like a god in my own universe—I had learned to manage, manipulate, and control others in my dreams. Sleep had become a drug for me, and I was hooked on it and started to sleep more, even taking naps to ensure I would get my high and stay in the world I totally had control over. But I didn't want to stop there. After researching more about lucid dreams, I had to go to the next step.

But in order to reach the next step, I had to do two things: the first was to wake in places that were familiar to me, rather than changing the scenery of wherever I was. Over the next few nights of thinking of such a place and falling asleep, I finally woke in my dream world, standing next to a pond that was identical to the pond and park in reality. And now, I was ready for the second thing to reach the next step.

I lay there thinking about Rae and was suddenly standing on the pier at the pond, looking out over the water. As I thought hard about her, a small blue circle of light appeared in front of me, making a circular motion around darkness. While concentrating harder, the circle grew brighter and larger until it was sizeable enough for someone to walk through.

I walked around to the other side. "Where are we going?" I heard Sally's voice first, and then her image came into focus, replacing the darkness inside the circle as she got into Rae's car.

"I figure we could go shopping for a while and then have lunch," Rae's voice responded; it was followed by her image. As I continued watching, the scene changed immediately from inside Rae's car to a clothing store when Rae said she needed a new outfit.

I couldn't believe it at first, but as far as I could tell, I truly was watching and hearing someone else's dream. I knew it wasn't my dream when I looked away from the portal and still saw the pond and park. Although I was able to see and hear what was going on in Rae's or Sally's dream—I didn't know which one it was—I felt as if I was standing in the shadows. Then, instantly, they were sitting at a table in a restaurant. Sally said, "I'm going to have the soup and salad."

"You think Frank will like this?" Rae asked Sally as she handed her a card.

"Frank?" I said out loud, without thinking.

"David?" Rae spoke my name after hearing my voice. She looked around but didn't see me in the restaurant. "I just swore I heard David," Rae told Sally, who hadn't heard me. I stepped through the circle, startling Rae as I suddenly appeared from nowhere. "Where did you come from?" she asked.

"You can see me?"

"Of course I can see you," she chuckled as we instantly stood outside her house. One of the things I noticed about dreamers is that if they aren't able to control their dreams, they will find themselves in different places quickly and seamlessly, as Rae had just done.

"Oh shit!" I spoke loudly, sitting up in my bed quickly. My heart raced inside me, and I wondered if I had made a dream connection with Rae.

The next night, I dropped Rae off early after our date. "Are you okay?" she asked. "What's your rush to get home?"

"I'm just tired and want to get some rest," I fibbed, and I kissed her.

"What's going on?" she said, sounding concerned. "You sure have been sleeping a lot over the last week or so."

I thought, *If you knew how right you are and did as I was doing, you might want to get rid of me early just so you could sleep.* I didn't want Rae to know, however, what I was doing just yet, so I assured her everything was fine and that I'd meet with her tomorrow.

Once I got home, I was eager to get to bed and get back to my dream world. I hoped to make contact with Rae again and find out what I could do inside her dreams. I lay there for hours trying to get to sleep. And then, as I looked into the portal that appeared in front of me and found myself staring into her dream, I wished I hadn't been in such a hurry that night to go to sleep.

I saw Rae kissing another guy, so, feeling discouraged, I waved my hand across the gateway to make it go away, and instantly, I was sitting on the edge of a cliff overlooking a large lake below in the valley. I knew it was just a dream she was having, but when I woke up, I still felt angry and betrayed.

When I picked her up in the morning, she noticed how silent I was on our way to school. "Are you upset with me?" Rae asked as I pulled into the school parking lot.

"No," I snapped, realizing I sounded harsh.

"Why are you biting my head off?" she asked.

Without thinking, I blurted out, "So who's the guy you were kissing?"

"*What?* What do you mean, the guy I was kissing? I wasn't kissing anyone."

I'd once again put my foot in my mouth because I hadn't separated the dream from reality.

"I don't like your accusation," she shouted at me. She then got out of the car, shouting, "Piss off!"

"Rae! Rae, please stop!" I called out as I chased after her.

She turned, hitting me in the chest. "Why would you even think I was kissing someone?"

"Rae, I'm sorry. It just came out."

"David, I went through this crap before, and I don't need it from you." She seemed calmer now but her tone was serious.

"Rae, it was only a dream that you had. But it seemed so real to me when I saw you kissing someone else."

She looked strangely at me. "A dream that *I* had?"

"Yes, last night. In your dream you were kissing someone else," I said.

Her mouth dropped open in disbelief. "You saw my dream?"

I couldn't blame her for doubting me, and now the conversation was out in the open, I didn't have a way of get out of telling her the truth. "Yes," I said nervously.

"Do you hear what you're saying?" she asked, laughing at me. "And besides, I don't remember what I dreamed last night. Maybe you had the dream. But I will tell you this: lately, you've been in a hurry to head home after our dates. You don't call as much as you did before." Her tone became serious as she said, "If I was dreaming about kissing someone else, maybe you need to pay more attention to me."

Ouch. Rae had me there. I was wrapped up in my life, regardless if it was reality or dreams, and I had stopped paying attention to her. She may have been having dreams about other guys because of it and not remembering them.

"And even if you can get into someone's dreams," she continued, "what gives you the right to do that?" She turned from me and went to her class.

As I stood there and thought about what Rae had just said, I wondered what *did* give me the right to peek into someone's dreams. Just because I had this gift, it didn't mean I should use it however I wanted. I'd invaded her dreams and her private world. And if she wanted to share a personal or intimate dream, then it was her choice to do it, not mine, by spying on her as she slept.

Later, Bobby, Steve, and I were talking as we ate lunch outside of the cafeteria. I didn't want them to know what I was doing in my dreams, but after Rae and Sally came over and sat down with us, I wasn't able to get away from the topic when Rae asked Bobby and Steve, "Did David tell you what he could do?"

"Rae, I thought about it, and you're right. I shouldn't have done that." I said, hoping she wouldn't say anymore.

"If I believed you could see inside my dreams, I would be upset," she said. "But since I don't believe it, I'm not. I just didn't like the idea of being accused of something I didn't do."

"What the hell are you two talking about?" Bobby asked, scratching his head in confusion.

"David says he can control his dreams," Rae giggled, "and even see inside other people's dreams while they sleep."

I felt my face flush. I have to admit; I did feel a little embarrassed about what I had told her.

"What did I dream last night?" Sally asked, also chuckling at me. "I'll give you a hundred dollars if you can tell me." She cocked her head at me. "Did I dream I was on a beautiful boat with big, strong men wearing Speedos who were waiting on me? Or maybe I was in a mud-wrestling tournament with a sexy girl you were drooling over," she said, poking fun at me as everyone else burst out laughing.

"Ha-ha," I said sourly. But after a few moments of their laughing and making comments at my expense, I decided to share my experience with them. I told them what I had done in dreams—how I knew I was dreaming; how I'd been able to stop the truck and everything in mid-action; how I tried different thoughts such as, sorcery, flying, and changing the direction of the dream; and even how I controlled the people. And then, I shared with them how I was able to get into Rae's dream by stepping through some type of a portal that came into being when I thought of her.

"You think I can make Lillie want me in her dreams?" Bobby asked, still laughing at me.

"I don't know. I know that inside my dreams I'm able to do anything to anyone I want. In Rae's dreams, however, I didn't try to make her do anything."

"And you better not," she spoke up.

"I guess in your dreams you could, but in Lillie's, I'm not sure," I responded seriously.

Bobby and especially Steve became more interested in the process as I continued telling them what they might be able to do with their dreams.

"Are you guys evening listening to yourselves?" Rae said, chuckling.

"How do you control them?" Steve asked, not paying attention to Rae.

"Well, it took me a few nights to get the hang of it, but once I realized I was in a dream, that's when I started experimenting with the different things I told you about."

Rae stood up and waved good-bye. "Okay, I'll talk to you guys later. Happy dreaming," she called over her shoulder as she and Sally walked away, still laughing at us.

Bobby studied me closely. "You're serious, aren't you?"

"Yes, I'm very serious. I'm able to make things happen in my dreams the way I want them—"

"Ladies!" Bobby interrupted. "What about the ladies?"

I didn't want to share with them the times that Rae and I spent together in my dreams, so I let them know that their dreams were their own, and there wasn't anything stopping them from dreaming whatever they wanted.

That night, I was sitting with Rae on her couch, talking about dreams in general—what we would like to have, see, and do in them. We talked about places to visit and even people we would like to see. But since Rae didn't believe me about controlling dreams, she still was thinking of dreams we could fulfill in reality, and that's why she was willing to listen as I explained the process of dream control.

What we didn't realize, as we sat on the couch, talking, was that Mary was upstairs on the balcony, listening intently. Mary's the type of girl who would try anything once, and she didn't have a problem understanding. What eventually took Bobby and Steve—and ultimately, Rae—about a week to learn, Mary mastered in one night.

Mary only thought of one person she wanted back into her life, regardless of whether it was a dream or not. She simply spoke one word quietly to herself: "Mom." With a hopeful heart as to what she could do to see her mom again, she continued listening, and after I finished telling my story, she got up from the floor and silently headed to her room to dream.

CHAPTER 3 DREAM EXPLORATION

Mary woke swinging in the backyard of a house. A creek was weaving in and out around the narrow road that led from her swing, flowing toward a small gathering of trees in the distance. She wore a white sundress and matching bonnet and white gloves. She headed toward the trees after seeing horses galloping into the forest. There were flowerbeds along the path, and she started picking different colored flowers, creating a bouquet as she went along.

As Mary reached the edge of the woods, the road disappeared, leaving only the creek for her to follow through the trees. Hearing sounds of the horses, she continued walking until she came to the clearing, where there was a cemetery. Still holding onto the bouquet, she walked past the tombstones that outlined the cemetery. Surrounded by trees with yellow blossoms was a heart-shaped white marble stone. With no other gravestones around to hide its view, she could see the waterfall flowing down the marker to the base, filling up the small pool of water where the creek ended.

She reached her hand out to move the red roses that grew around the grave, and a thorn pricked her finger, causing a drop of blood to spill into the pond, mixing with the water. She watched as the red-colored water came out from the top of the waterfall and headed back down the marker. As it reached the center of the heart-shaped tombstone, it changed the white marble to red, and cracks started appearing, hiding the name of the person buried in the grave.

In slow motion the grave marker shattered into pieces, and Mary fell on her knees and started weeping.

"Why are you crying?" a woman's voice asked softly. Mary looked around the cemetery but didn't see anyone; then she heard the voice again. "Why are you crying, child?" the voice asked with sympathy as a slight breeze blew around Mary.

"The tombstone is smashed," Mary answered with sadness.

"Yes, but why should that upset you?"

"It was my mother's tombstone," Mary answered, feeling heartbroken as she turned her attention back to the marker that lay in rubble on the ground.

"Your mother's?" the voice chuckled. "No, child, that's not your mother's grave. There's no one there. If someone was, the tombstone would still be standing, and the roses would be blooming."

Mary looked at the roses she just moved aside and saw they were no longer bright red; they were fading and dying. She then looked at her bouquet, and it too was fading of the bright colors. "Where's my mother?" Mary asked, feeling alone and angry.

"Your mother?" the voice said. "Child, she's the one who brought you here. Don't you see her?" The voice had a curious tone, not understanding why Mary couldn't see her mother.

"No, I don't," Mary cried.

"Look in the pool of water," the voice said.

Mary looked down in the water. "I can't see her," she re-sponded in frustration as she tried to see through reddish water.

"Look again and see," the voice chuckled.

Mary watched as the water twirled when the wind blew over it, causing the red to fade and revealing crystal-clear water. As Mary looked at her reflection in the water, the breeze came again, and Mary no longer saw herself but her mother's face, smiling back from the water. "Mom?" She questioned the manifestation gazing up at her. "Is it you?" Her excitement grew as her heart pounded inside her. Reaching her hand toward the water, Mary caressed the image of her mom—and then, suddenly, she was standing in a field of daisies, caressing her mother's face.

"Yes, dear. It's me," her mom responded, filling the air around them with her soft voice.

Mary hugged her and said, "But I don't understand. Why did the tombstone crumble?"

"I've always been here, Mary. Inside of you," her mom said as she touched Mary's face with love. And then her mom vanished from view, leaving Mary standing in the field alone.

Mary started to cry because her mom had left. She looked back toward the ruins of the tombstone and saw a smaller marker in its place. Walking over to the gravesite, she reached out her hand to touch the stone, but the marker dissolved instantly, showing no trace that a grave was even there. Mary realized she was dreaming. "Mom, you're here with me." As she spoke the words, her mother stood in front of her again. "It worked," Mary said softly as she reached for her mother's hand ... and both of them faded.

Mary woke up, crying in bed as she thought about her mom. She knew that it was only a dream, but she also felt that now, anytime she wanted to be with her mom, all she had to do was to dream of her. Mary spent many nights in her dream world with her mother. She would create worlds where they would spend countless hours, living a life Mary dreamed.

Steve, on the other hand, had tried many times to realize he was dreaming without success. As he would wake from a dream, he became angry that he couldn't realize he was dreaming in a dream. He would lie in bed, struggling to forget how bad his life was, only to fall asleep and wake up to nightmares instead of dreams. He wanted so much to find some kind of happiness inside his dreams; he started taking his foster mother's sleeping pills, just to stay asleep longer, thinking it would help.

And then, finally, while walking along the countryside in the rain, Steve found himself looking at the farmhouses in the distance, wondering what type of people lived in such an isolated place. Being wet and chilled from the cold rain, he headed to one of the houses. He climbed through an old fence that marked the boundary lines of the farms and continued walking, but he soon became aware that the more he walked toward the house, the farther away it became. "What the hell?" he questioned as he saw the scenery moving.

As the wind picked up and it started raining harder, the fields began to flood, leaving him standing in water just above his ankles. He started running toward the house, and after what seemed like hours of running and becoming out of breath, he realized he could no longer see the house. When he stopped to catch his breath, he saw there weren't any homes around. He dropped to his knees in the water and mud. "Where the hell are you?" he cried aloud, feeling isolated.

"We're right here, honey," a woman's voice spoke from behind him.

Turning to see who was talking, he saw a woman and man sitting on the porch of a house a few yards from him. "Who are you?" he asked. He got up from the ground that was no longer wet and muddy but filled with green grass and dry to the touch.

"Who are we?" the man said, laughing at Steve. "What game are you playing today?"

"Okay, sweetie, time to stop playing games and get ready for the picnic," the woman told Steve and then took a sip of tea.

"You can't have a picnic in ..." Steve stopped speaking as he looked up into the sky. "Where's ... the storm?" Steve said in a low voice.

"Storm?" the man and woman asked at the same time as they got out of their rocking chairs to look up at the blue sky.

"Just as I thought," the man sighed.

"I know, honey," the woman said. "Another day without rain. Oh, well. More tea, dear?" She turned to Steve as she lifted the pitcher. "I don't suppose you want any tea, do you, dear?" Before he could respond, she said, "Oh, my," as she saw the jug was no longer filled with tea but muddy water.

Steve blinked his eyes and found himself alone in the rain, back in the fields, where the floodwaters now reached up past his waist. As he tried desperately to move through the water and onto a hill just ahead of him, he slipped beneath the water. Struggling to catch his breath, he moved a glass of water away from his mouth, gasping for air.

"Steve, don't drink so fast," a woman said, as he found himself sitting at a kitchen table with a glass of water in his hand.

"Where am I?" he questioned in confusion as he looked around the room.

"Why, you're here," another voice said from behind him. Looking back to see who it was, he heard still another voice say, "No, you're here." As he kept looking around, different people and places appeared to him, just as fast as they were saying, "You're here. No, you're here."

"Stop!" Steve shouted at the top of his lungs, raising his hands to the sky as he stood in the field once more. "I said, stop!" he shouted again as the floodwaters were reaching his neck. "Please, stop," he sobbed ... and he was lying on the ground in front of the grayish farmhouse where he had met the man and woman on the porch. "You're a dream," he kept saying over and over as he lay in the fetal position on his bed.

In his dream, Steve felt the same way he felt in reality: alone, drowning, and being passed from one place to another without catching his breath in between. His life seemed to go nowhere with each new foster parent. The same nightmare that Steve woke from that night was the beginning of his understanding of dreams as he spoke the words "You're a dream," over and over.

Every time he would go to sleep, he'd wake up in his dream world, sitting in the rocker on the porch by himself at the old farmhouse, looking out at the empty fields that surrounded him—that is, he did until he learned to create what he desired.

Bobby didn't want such a simple life as Steve had in dreams. He needed the excitement that life gave him, a life that was busy with places and people.

He stood on the corner, trying to cross a busy street, and the only sounds he could hear were the words he spoke while waiting for the light to change. Others walked by, moving their lips but producing no sounds. It wasn't just the people he saw that were silent but also the vehicles, animals, and even low-flying planes as he looked past the skyscrapers toward the yellowish clouds rolling across the blue sky.

"Hey, you can go now." A lone voice spoke to him in a noiseless world. He looked down to see a young boy pointing to the crossing guard in the middle of the street, who was waving for him to cross. As Bobby walked past the guard, he saw she was blowing a whistle that gave no sound while she continued waving other pedestrians across. He continued watching her until he bumped into an older man on the other side of the street.

"Hey, watch where you're going," the man said angrily, as the world suddenly came alive with sounds of humanity in the city streets.

"Sorry for bumping into you," Bobby said with embarrassment.

"What?" the man said loudly to Bobby.

Bobby once again told the man he was sorry, but Bobby couldn't hear his own voice as he spoke the words. Paranoia started to overcome him, and he ran down the street, frantically trying to find someone who could hear him. And then, just as the noises around the city began getting louder, they suddenly went quiet, and he stood in the middle of the street with hundreds of people approaching him from all sides.

As he turned around in circles, seeing everyone around, he was unable to hear them talking. The same young boy approached Bobby, smiled, and handed him a record, and then he walked back toward the crowd, which moved, creating a path for the boy. Watching the boy, Bobby saw him walk up to the music store, waving at Bobby to follow as he went inside the store.

While Bobby stood there, contemplating what to do, one side of the crowd moved closer to him, forcing him to move in the direction of the boy, until he finally reached the door of the music store. Looking inside, he saw the young boy standing next to a DJ's table. Bobby looked at the record in his hand and smiled as he walked into the store.

Bobby turned on the music, and slowly he started to hear as his head started bobbing and his fingers tapped on the table. "Much better," Bobby said, but once again, he was unable to hear his own words. Each tone got louder and faster, and he saw the crowd gathering outside the record store. Letting the music play, he left the store and went back into the streets. More and more people came into view from nowhere, dancing to the music that reached all over the city. "Oh, man, this has got to be a dream!" Bobby shouted.

"Shut up down there!" a woman shouted from a window above the record store.

"You can hear me?" he said excitedly, glad he'd found someone who could hear him.

"You're crazy," she replied and then slammed the window.

As Bobby continued to dance with the crowd, he saw a nice-looking young lady in the multitude of people. He waved his hands toward the shop, and the music switched from fast to slow. He and she took to the streets alone, dancing as they moved along its route. "David was right. This looks and feels so real," Bobby told the lady, who didn't say anything but just smiled.

"You called me?" I asked Bobby, as the portal between our dreams opened after he spoke my name.

"How did you get here?" Bobby asked as I stood alongside him in the street. "Shit, she's gone," he said, displeased when he realized the woman he was with no longer stood there, and the music had stopped playing.

"Sorry," I said, smiling.

"Why did all the people leave?" he asked.

"I'm thinking I startled you, and you lost your concentration on the dream. I'm surprised you didn't wake up because of it."

"How did you get here?" he inquired.

"I was in my own dream when I heard you say my name. I was able to make a dream connection with you, just like when I told you that I was in Rae's dream," I explained.

"So I'm really dreaming, then?" Bobby said.

"Yep. And by the looks of it," I said, observing the scenery in his dream, "not much is going on here."

"If you're telling the truth, I should be able to change that," he responded, chuckling. "Let's go for a ride," he said, and then instantly an orange Corvette was in the middle of the street. "Oh, hell yeah!" he said and opened the door. "This is *my* ride," he told strangers who passed by as they started to appear, filling up the city. "You coming?" he asked me.

"No, I was about to help Rae in her dreams," I informed him, and I disappeared into a portal I had just created, thinking of Rae.

"Suit yourself," he said, laughing as he climbed into the car. And then he sped down the street.

While Bobby was enjoying his newfound freedom in his car, I went to find Rae in her dreams.

Rae walked along the shores of the sea in the coolness of fall, enjoying the breeze, watching people play on the beach, and waving to the boaters who passed by. When night came, she sat on an old tree stump next to a fire, talking with her friends and watching the moon's reflection in the water.

Suddenly, Jack appeared and found a seat next to her. "How you been?" he asked Rae, as sparks from the fire rose above them and disappeared into the night sky.

"What are you doing here?" she asked, avoiding Jack's eyes.

"Can't we at least be friends and just enjoy the evening and talk?"

"Talk?" she said angrily. "You want to talk? I tried talking to you, and you ignored me and went off with someone else. Why would you even think I'd want to talk with you?" She got up and started walking down the beach, but Jack followed a few feet behind.

"How many times do I have to say I'm sorry?" he wailed. "I keep telling you I'm sorry."

"Sorry! You're sorry?" She turned around and slapped him. "You asshole! You were hitting on my best friend, and now you're sorry?" she said and continued down the beach.

"That was a long time ago, Rae. Haven't you ever done something you're sorry for?"

Stopping in her tracks, she glared at Jack with hatred in her eyes. "Yes, I've done something I was sorry about. In fact, I even regret it. I'm sorry I ever dated you; that's what I'm sorry about!" Jack wasn't sure what to say, and as he fumbled for words, Rae continued, "You were kissing Carmen and making advances toward her. How can I ever forgive you for that?"

"Rae, I'm very sorry for what happened," Jack told her as he reached into his pocket and pulled out a small ring box. "And to prove it, I got you something."

She looked at the box and was filled with anticipation. She held her hands to her mouth, trying to contain her excitement. "Is that what I think it is?"

As she reached for the box, Jack opened it, revealing an engagement ring. He promised he would never hurt her again, and then asked, "Will you marry me?"

Just as she was about to respond, Rae looked over his shoulders toward her friends still sitting around the fire—and saw herself walking with me in the distance. She shook her head, muttering, "This can't be right." She looked back at Jack, touched his face, and watched him disappear as I walked up to her. "I'm dreaming, aren't I?" Rae asked.

"Yes, I thought you might need help realizing you were dreaming, so I came to you in your dream," I said.

"You bastard!" she shouted and pushed me away from her.

"What the hell is that for?" I didn't understand the sudden angry response from her.

"You were spying on me in my dreams. What gives you the right?"

"Rae, I didn't know you were here. You and I were holding hands, walking along the beach. Then I saw you with Jack. I thought I was in your dream and that I could help you learn dream control. That's what we talked about before we went to sleep tonight."

She seemed to be thinking about my response and remembered that before we went to sleep, she in fact did say I could help in her dream if I was able to. "David, how can I have two dreams at the same time with two different people?"

"I don't know," I admitted. "Maybe you were in Jack's dream."

"If I was in Jack's dream, how could he be gone, and I'm still here?"

I shook my head. "I really don't know."

She looked around and then smiled slyly. "I can do whatever I want?"

"Yes, anything you desire," I told her.

As we stood there on the beach, Rae closed her eyes, and I watched as her dream world change from place to place and time to time. The longer she closed her eyes, the faster we moved through her dream world. One moment I stood there, seeing houses in a subdivision; next it was skyscrapers in cities, country homes by the ocean, and even castles out of the Middle Ages. Rae had changed landscapes so fast I wasn't able to keep up with her, and I saw her disappear just before I woke up to the ringing sound of my cell phone.

"Yeah," I answered wearily.

"David, it worked! It really worked!" Rae said with excitement in her voice.

I felt dizzy and nauseated. "What?" I asked, not understanding her.

"Hurry up and pick me up for school, and I'll tell you about it," she said and then hung up the phone.

On the way to school we talked, and Rae said she was able to change her dream world and be in different places at once. But what she found out was that it wasn't all at once; it was just that she was changing them so fast they seemed to be one. "That's the reason I saw you walking with me and coming toward Jack and me. When I started dreaming and not liking what the dream was, I was able to change it through my mind to something else," she said excitedly.

"I'm lost," I told her.

"I had a dream that you and I were walking along the beach and you were trying to help me gain control of my dream. Once I understood what you meant, I dreamed something else. And that's how it came to Jack and me, standing on the beach. That was another dream, a kind of a dream within a dream."

"So you decided to dream of Jack?" I asked.

"No, I fell into another dream, which had Jack in it, and when I saw you, and I didn't like the dream with Jack, I slipped back into my first dream of you and me—that's when Jack vanished, and you were standing next to me." She spoke as if she had been doing this for a very long time.

I was still confused. "But how do you know what dream is the real dream?" I asked.

"Real dream, David? What's a real dream? Besides, does it matter if it's a real or fake dream? Isn't it all just dreams any-way?" she chuckled.

I shrugged, not knowing what to say. "I guess."

"The point is that I realized I was dreaming in the dream with Jack when I saw you and me together. I was able to bring the two dreams together, and I think that's why Jack and the other me, who was with you, disappeared."

I was still dumbfounded. All I could think of was that when I first started telling my friends I could control my dreams, it was Rae who'd said, "Are you guys even listening to yourselves?" And now, I was the one who couldn't believe what she was tell-ing me.

"Don't ask me how I did it, but you wouldn't believe the dreams I've gone through just in one night," she said. "It's like I can take an object from one dream and place it into another. The best part of it is, I don't have to go to sleep for the second dream."

After Rae had learned to control her dreams, the four of us set out to learn dream world. We spent many hours dream-ing. For weeks my friends and I dreamed and controlled many aspects in our dream worlds. And anytime we wanted to see someone's dream, we would concentrate on that person and soon be in that person's dreams. But out of respect for each other in our dreams, we would call the person's name to gain access into the dream through a dream portal, as if we were walking through a door in reality. Rae didn't like the idea of just going into someone's dream, but after a while she too was curious about her other friend's dreams.

Waving good-bye to Bobby and I in dream world, Rae opened a portal. She stood instantly in the doorway of a bar. She walked past other patrons and looked around; finally, she found herself sitting with Sally at a table next to the dance floor. "I'm in Sally's dream," Rae smiled, seeing her best friend was having a dream with her in it.

"Ladies, are you ready for the night of your life?" came the announcer's voice through the speakers filling the lounge. Rae realized Sally was dreaming of male dancers at a nightclub. Not wanting to miss anything, Rae spoke something, and she was immediately sitting at the table where her other self was.

"What do you think?" Sally asked.

"I'm going to enjoy this night," Rae responded and then said, "Oh, my gosh!" Rae's eyes were wide open as the male dancer started dancing around the stage, stripping off some of his clothes to the sound of the music.

"Whoa. Yeah!" Sally screamed, along with other customers.

"I can't believe I'm staying here," Rae told Sally, giggling at her situation.

"Why?" Sally looked concerned but still cheerful as an article of clothing fell onto their table.

"Nothing," Rae responded, waving the dropped shorts around in the air. Getting into the mood, Rae also started cheering on the dancers.

Bobby soon vanished into a gateway of his own, only to find some dreams are just strange. Bobby materialized on top of a hill and immediately took cover behind large rocks when he heard explosions around him. Peering from behind the boulders, he looked down into the valley, where he saw firebombs falling from the sky and exploding around people who were fleeing to a cave opening. *What the hell's going on?* he thought in disbelief of what he was watching.

Bobby found cover behind boulders along the way as he faded in and out while trying to reach the cave, where he vanished inside the entrance. Finding Tealo, his cousin, just inside the entrance, Bobby ran over to him, scared and sweaty as he tried to catch his breath. "Tealo, are you okay?" Bobby asked in horror as the explosions kept ringing outside the cave entrance.

"Cuz!" Tealo smiled when he saw Bobby.

As the explosions continued outside the entrance, Bobby saw men, women, and children climbing down ladders into the cave floor.

"Where is everyone going?" Bobby asked.

"You're kidding, right?" Tealo shouted, pointing out toward the valley as another explosion nearly came in the entrance.

Bobby went to the mouth of the cave and watched more fireballs continuing to fall around the area. Bobby pointed toward the fireballs as they started coming closer. "Watch," Bobby said. Just then, bolts of lightning raced from each of Bobby's fingers, destroying the firebombs in midair. As more and more explosions occurred in the air, the fallout lit up the sky, creating the illusion of falling stars. "Not too bad," Bobby said proudly, chuckling as he turned to look at Tealo.

"Great. Now we've got to start all over," Tealo said, clearly upset with Bobby.

"What?" Bobby asked in confusion.

"Now we have to start all over again," Tealo said, and then Bobby woke up as an explosion hit where he was standing. He looked around his room and shook his head.

"People's dreams are just not right," he told himself as he lay back down on the bed.

Tealo's dream was one of many dreams in which we learned how dreamers went along inside their dreams, having no knowledge of what was truly going on until they woke. But one of the benefits of controlling dreams was that *we* no longer were confused about what was going on inside of dreams. Just as others like Tealo were sleeping and letting the dream take its course, we did something about ours to ensure we had a great experience. And Mary was no exception to Rae, Bobby, Steve, and me.

After learning to be a Lucider and spending time with her mom, she started creating nightmares for herself, just to learn to control anything that came her way. And she was so much into dream world, she started wearing the clothes that matched the life she was living in dreams.

Mary wore a bright blue long dress that a queen might have worn in the Middle Ages. She wore her coal-black hair in a ponytail, with a tiara on her head, as she created a dream world filled with snow-peaked mountains, green valleys, and crystal-clear rivers that ran through a dense forest. Satisfied with her creation, she climbed upon the unicorn and headed through the forest toward the valley where she had created a large creature.

Riding on the path, she listened to many different animals that made the forest their home. Looking around and feeling uneasy about the surrounding, she took the sword that rested inside a sheath hanging on her unicorn and lifted it up in front of her, waiting for the creature to strike at any moment. Upon hearing the strange noise, the unicorn reared up and started running faster down the path that led out of the woods.

Mary finally got her unicorn under control in time to prevent herself from falling down the edge of the cliff. She sat there looking across the valley below. "I see you," she said as she watched the trees in the valley swaying back and forth. She lifted up her sword and pointed it at the path the creature had just made in the forest, and instantly, she faded from the edge of the cliff and stood just behind the figure.

"I'm over here!" Mary called out with authority in her voice. Coming back out of the brush and trees and floating just above the ground, the creature, wearing a red robe and hood, concealed its face from Mary. Standing as tall as Mary sitting on her unicorn, it lifted its arm, revealing its hairy hand and stubby fingers. Multicolored lights shot toward Mary, only to hit the force field around her. "That can't be your best," Mary said, enticing the creature to strike again.

Just as the creature lifted its hand again and fire flew in her direction, Mary vanished and reappeared behind the creature. "You missed again," she said, taunting the creature. As the creature turned around to look at her, she stuck the sword in the ground and spoke a few words under her breath. Watching the beam of light come from the end of the golden handle of the sword, she reached her hand over it and caught some of the light.

The light moved like a small snake around her fingers, and she caused the world she created to vanish, leaving only the creature and her standing in the middle of a desert. Mary wasn't trying to hurt the creature. She was learning how to control herself when she was faced with something and how to control her powers as she moved from dream world to dream world.

Unlike Mary, who was able to think of different sceneries and be there instantly, I used gateways to go through dream worlds.

I lifted myself up in the air as I thought about flying. I floated through gateways, looking at dreams I created instantly. I didn't like any particular dream I was seeing, so I thought about Jack and then vanished into a portal that led me to his dream. As I floated above the ground, I could see him driving his car, heading outside of town into the country.

Jack stopped the car at the edge of a lake. When he got out of the car, I saw he was wearing a black tux and top hat as he opened the rear car door. He pulled out a basket and then ran around to the passenger side of the car and opened the door. Rae emerged from the car, wearing a pink formal dress.

"He's dreaming about Rae again," I muttered to myself as I landed just behind them in trees. Although I didn't like the situation, I followed them as they headed toward the water. I didn't like Jack, and I was envious when I saw that he brought along a basket of food and a blanket.

As I watched them eat lunch, I started wondering if it was Rae's dream I was watching. I thought about contacting Rae to find out, but knowing she would be upset with me, I figured it would be better to let it go. After all, I did think of Jack's dream instead of Rae. But seeing them together, my jealousy started to take over as they lay there on the blanket, enjoying the sun.

I couldn't understand why they were dressed so formally. And from my own experiences in other people's dreams I learned anything could happen, even the strangest things. And then, all of a sudden, they both were in the water, swimming naked. Of course I couldn't stand for it. And I should have left it alone and moved to another dream, but I couldn't.

Floating back up into the sky, I flew above them without them knowing. Waving my hand across the scene of the dream, thunderclouds started forming in the distance. As the winds picked up, their basket and blanket started flying like debris along with Jack's clothes. Just as Jack was about to reach for his clothes, I set them ablaze. As he started running toward the car, the rain started pouring down on him alone, and I then changed the car into a horse and buggy without a top. I placed the buggy in the middle of a busy street, where onlookers honked at him as they passed.

I woke up smiling as I thought of Jack's embarrassment of being naked in the middle of a street in the rain. I messed with Jack's dream out of spite. But I wasn't the only person directing dreams. Steve also was changing dreams. But his was more out of hatred than meanness.

Steve became more skilled in the crafts he learned in dreams. And with this new knowledge, he wanted revenge on the people he felt had hurt him over the years. That night, Steve decided to pay back John Stier for all the things he had done to Steve.

Sitting in the living room of his dream home, Steve thought about the night John had kicked him when he was lying on the ground. Steve started visualizing John, and a gateway to John's dream finally opened up. Stepping through the door that lead to John's dream, Steve saw him playing pool in a rundown pool hall.

When Steve walked over to John, John looked at him and said, "Two hundred to play," and then made two balls in the pocket at the same time.

"Sure," Steve replied, "but I want the stakes to be a thousand or more." He tossed a wad of money next to the cue ball. "And you can go first."

John looked at Steve oddly and agreed.

Steve waited for his turn as he watched John instead of the game.

"You're up," John said after missing his fourth shot.

Steve missed his first shot on purpose and then sat back down.

"Might just be the easiest thousand I made all day," John said as he set up his next shot. As he continued to make the shots, John looked at Steve after each shot and grinned after each ball fell into the pockets of the table, until he finally got to the eight ball.

"Another thousand?" Steve asked before John took the last shot to win the game.

"Are you serious?" John laughed when he looked at the cue ball a few inches from the eight ball, next to the side pocket.

"Let's make it another two." Steve responded, smiling.

"Your loss," John said. After calling the side pocket, sure he would win, John hit the cue ball—and Steve moved his hand, preventing the cue ball from hitting the eight ball. "Son of a bitch," John swore, as onlookers wondered how he could have missed the eight ball.

Steve went back up to the table, and with all of his pool balls still on the table, he named each pocket they would go into and then named where the eight ball would fall. Laughing at him, John shook his head and sat down.

With one stroke of the cue stick, every ball fell into every pocket, just as Steve had called. After knocking in the last ball, the cue ball rolled slowly next to the eight ball at the wrong end of the table. Without stopping, the cue ball started spinning faster until it exploded, knocking the eight back to the other end of the table, where in fell it into the pocket Steve had called.

"You bastard! You hustled my ass!" John shouted, about to hit Steve with a cue stick. But as soon as John lifted his cue stick in the air, he found himself standing on the sidewalk in the dark, watching himself kicking Steve. As he continued to watch the beating he was giving Steve, he fell to his knees, screaming in pain each time his other John-self kicked Steve.

Standing in front of him, Steve pulled John's head by his hair and forced him to watch the kicks and feel the pain. Steve spoke hatefully in John's face. "Look at me, you son of a bitch. I want you to know who's doing this to you. And I will ensure that every time you go to sleep, you will spend the last few moments of your dreams in the same agony you put me through."

As Steve talked to him, John stared to fade. "Not yet, you bastard!" Steve said preventing John from waking up. "You're going to feel every kick, every hit, and every pain you caused me."

John continued to scream in pain, shouting to his other self to stop hitting and kicking Steve. And just as he was about to wake up naturally, Steve whispered, "Remember this," in John's ear before he vanished from view. John awoke fearfully as he thought about the pain he had in his dream.

Over time, Steve made his promise stick. He waited in his own dream for John to sleep. And when he finally did, Steve brought John back to the same sidewalk, feeling the pain with every kick. After a while, in reality, when Steve saw John, he noticed a change in John. Whenever John saw Steve at school or any other place, Steve saw the same fear in John's eyes that he'd had in his dreams. Steve had found a way affected a person's reality from dream world.

Because Steve had acquired this new gift, he was staying away from us more often in dreams. We encountered him from time to time, only to see him become more secretive, fading in and out of our dreams as if he was one of the dreamers. But at this time, it didn't matter if Steve wanted to be around us in dreams or not; we were enjoying our dreams.

"I'll race you," Rae said as she got on her horse and headed along the pasture. Leaving our picnic food on the blanket next to the creek, I climbed on my horse and rode after her, listening to her laughter as I got closer. While looking back at me, she smiled, and the wind blew her hair around her face as her horse switched from a gallop to a run, heading toward the hills on the horizon.

Spurring my horse, I caught up with her when we came up to the hills that rolled out in front of us. We rode along the green hills until we found part of the creek flowing peacefully in front of us. "Next time," I told her when the horses stopped to drink from the creek, "I'll win."

"This is beautiful," Rae said as she looked around, enjoying the serenity that encompassed us. She looked back at me as I stared at her, watching the breeze gently move her hair from side to side. "What?"

"Nothing." I smiled and climbed down off my horse. I helped her down, and we walked over and sat on rocks along the creek, watching sparkles dance and shine in the water from the sun. I don't like to lose, so I left Rae to her thoughts, and I climbed on my horse and shouted, "I'll race you back!" As I headed down the hills toward our picnic area, I heard her shouting after me, "You wuss! You're scared to race me fairly?"

I rode along the bottom of the hills and slowed my horse to a gallop when I saw two dirt bikes heading our direction. This was Rae's and my dreams merged together, and no one was supposed to be here.

"Who's that?" Rae asked as she stopped her horse next to mine.

"I'm not sure, but they seem to be in a hurry to get over here," I responded.

"Maybe they're just riders, out having a good time," she replied, trying to ease my mind.

"I didn't bring any dreamers along, did you?" I asked, as they got closer.

We heard the revving of their dirt bikes get louder as they started jumping over sand mounds that suddenly appeared all around us. "Tell me you just changed the scenery, Rae," I said, feeling the panic inside of me well up. I climbed down to hold the horses, as they were getting startled from the bikes. The riders circled us, and I raised my hand, planning to either stop the dream or go on the defense.

"David, don't!" Rae shouted, stopping the ball of fire ready to leave my hands.

The riders stopped their bikes just front of us, and one of them took off his helmet.

"You should have seen your face!" Bobby said, laughing.

"What the hell! You scared the shit out of us," I told him angrily.

"Hey, man, you talk to her," Bobby replied, pointing to Rae.

"Got you," Rae said, smiling. "And what do you mean, *scared us*?" Rae saw me standing there with a half-smile, "Oh, don't be so uptight."

"I'm not. I thought we weren't going to just pop into each other's dreams without letting each other know." I spoke in my defense for being a little worried.

"I called Bobby when I was at the creek, waiting on your slowpoke ass," Rae said, still unable to stop smiling.

"But you should have seen your face," Bobby said, still chuckling.

"You'll get your turn," I said, pushing on his shoulder.

"Who's that?" Rae asked, looking at the other person still on the bike and still wearing a helmet. Smiling at us, Bobby waved the person over.

"Lillie?" I asked with surprise after she removed her helmet.

"How did she get here?" Rae asked Bobby.

"Well, I figured if I had to wait on you to let me know when to play the joke, I was going to have some company." Bobby smiled at Lillie.

After talking for a while and just enjoying our dream we shared together, we started riding again. Bobby and Lillie were in front of us on their dirt bikes, but soon faded in the distance, and Rae galloped into a mist, disappearing a few moments later.

Too bad it's only a dream, I thought as I started vanishing from dreams, back to reality.

We explored many dreams as we continued learning whatever we could. But after some time, the excitement started wearing off, and things we did were starting to bore us. We controlled our own worlds and others inside of theirs, and there weren't any surprises left. We lost a lot of the excitement we first had at the beginning, until one day we were sitting at the pond in reality, and the four of us were talking. It was after that day that we were caught up in our dreams with no way out, as we soon discovered what Steve had been doing in his dreams.

CHAPTER 4 IRREVERSIBLE DREAMS

We were sitting at the pond, telling each other stories of what we did when we weren't sharing dreams together. "What about you?" Steve asked me.

Smiling at Rae, I thought about how we would walk along beaches on our private island or go horseback riding. We even visited the Eiffel Tower a couple of times. We would also create scenes of ancient worlds, such as Egypt and Rome, where we would role-play as pharaohs and queens in Egypt and enjoy toga parties in Rome.

We found the one thing that helped us a lot in our dreams—if we wanted to meet someone or visit some place we'd never been before, we'd concentrate on pictures of the person or place to get the image in our minds. Then, in dreams, we would enjoy what we wanted to do. It may not have been how reality was at those places, but it was close enough for us to enjoy ourselves.

When I wasn't spending time with Rae, I would ride my mo-torcycle across dream worlds, jumping through portals as fast as I could think of them. I also learned how to scuba dive, which gave me the opportunity to hunt for treasures in the deep seas without worrying about sharks. For me, it was much easier to learn things in dreams than in reality. Besides, I didn't have the money to pay for all the things I did in my dreams.

"If you two don't stop spending so much time together in your dreams, you won't want to be together in reality much longer," Bobby said, grasping at why I looked dreamily at Rae. "Me, on the other hand," Bobby said, "I've created a place I could go and have fun without constantly changing dreams. I don't mind exploring now and then, but I'd rather sit in one place and have things come to me."

"How's that? You're not much of a homebody person in reality. Why would you want to be one in dreams?" Rae asked, finding it hard to believe he wasn't trying to conquer worlds and have more dreams of women.

"Well, I have a mansion," he said and then he started chuckling. "I really have about half a dozen. I change them from time to time, depending on who I have in my dream. When I dream and I'm not doing anything with you guys, I head straight for my mansion. Once I'm there, then I figure out what I want to do. But most of the time it's having parties and swimming in the pool, enjoying the good life I don't have in realty."

"Mr. Playboy of dreams," Rae said, giggling.

"Mr. Playboy. I like the sound of that," Bobby said.

"And you?" I asked Steve, trying to figure out what he did in his dreams since he seemed to be secretive about them.

"I have my own place too. It's a farmhouse in the country."

"Farmhouse?" Bobby said, surprised. "What the hell you want with a farmhouse?" Bobby didn't know why anyone would want a plain old house instead of the Taj Mahal of dreams.

"It suits me," Steve responded almost coldly.

"Okay, but I think you're missing out on the fun," Bobby replied, shaking his head.

"I've grown accustomed to the isolation it gives," Steve said. "In fact, I like it a lot. And not only that, when I want people around, I just start thinking of dreamers. When the portal opens up for me to see their dreams, I usually merge their dream into mine to keep me entertained."

"Entertained?" Rae asked, only to get a smile from Steve in response.

We weren't sure exactly what Steve meant by "entertained," but we figured if that's how he wanted to spend time in dreams, that was his business. Rae on the other hand, enjoyed creating fun dreams for little children. She would concentrate on four or five kids around the neighborhood and then visit their dreams. If she saw they weren't having a good dream, she'd merge them into hers and create an amusement park or something else. When I asked her about it once, she just told me it made her happy, doing good.

However, she wasn't always that nice to dreamers. She told me once, and I'm sure she did it more often than what she led me to believe, that she'd visit Sally in her dream. Often, Sally dreamed of winning a beauty contest. That didn't bother Rae; in fact, she told me she used dream magic to persuade one of the judges. But as it turned out, Sally started becoming vain about her looks; she started treating the other girls as trash in her dreams.

Naturally, that didn't sit too well with Rae, so at the last possible moment, when the announcer was about to call Sally's name as the winner, Rae caused a pimple to grow from Sally's cheek until it exploded on the judges and the announcer. Rae used her gift again to have a recount, and then the announcer called someone else's name, leaving Sally humiliated.

And the best thing about that particular dream was that when Rae was talking with Sally a day or so later, Sally told Rae how she was dreaming about a beauty contest and won. Since Sally was unaware of Rae being a Lucider, Rae didn't have the heart to ask her about the pimple. However, when Sally would get a blemish on her face, Rae would ask, "Do you think the judge would let you win with that?"—just to remind Sally of how the dream truly did go.

We continued trying to figure out new ways we could entertain ourselves within dream world. Some of the ideas we had were interesting. We would create a world and place dreamers in it, just to watch what they would do. We even thought of a plan to ensure they reentered into the dream where they left off, remembering everything they had done, to make it one long story.

Other ideas were just downright devilish. We talked about having wars against each other by using dreamers as combatants, fighting one another until everyone was dead or—to put it better—they woke up. But even those ideas didn't seem to spark an interest to keep us occupied.

We wanted something more than practical jokes on each other or on dreamers. We wanted something that would make a name for ourselves, not only in dream world but also in reality itself. After all, we felt we were the only ones who were able to control the new frontiers of dreams, and we were ready to use this power any way we could.

Just as I'd gotten the god mentality when I first started, I could tell by our conversations that my friends were now swallowed up in a world as I had been. I saw the gleam in their eyes as they thought about what they'd done and what they were planning to do. They had tasted the drug of dreams I'd given them, and they wanted more each night as they closed their eyes to enter the magical world of make-believe that was now their reality.

"Has anyone tried controlling a person's reality by using his or her dreams to do it?" Bobby finally spoke up.

I wondered if the others were thinking as I did. Could people be controlled in reality by their dreams? None of us was able to answer Bobby at first, but we sat there feeling intrigued by the possibilities of what we might have at our fingertips.

"What?" Bobby said seriously when he saw our expressions. "You guys telling me I'm the first to think about that?"

"No, but I think you just might be the first to admit it," I replied, smiling at Rae and Steve.

"You ass," Bobby said and chuckled after realizing that I too had thought as he did. "You're just as bizarre as me."

Bobby proceeded to tell us that he spent a lot of his dreams with Lillie and was trying to figure a way to move her desire for him from dreams to reality.

"Lillie?" Rae questioned Bobby after hearing the stories of him and other girls in his pool.

"Yes. Lillie," he replied defensively. He was annoyed that Rae seemed to disapprove of what he was thinking.

"And you think interfering with her dreams is going to do it?" Rae sneered.

"I don't know. I thought that's what we're trying to figure out—new ways to have fun in dreams."

"Yes, have fun," Rae agreed. "Not be an ass." When Bobby's face revealed his hurt at her words, she quickly said, "Bobby, I'm so sorry." After accepting her apology, they both took a deep breath, reflecting on how fast their lives had been changing. "And you're right," Rae said, feeling bad for speaking sharply to him.

"What about you?" I asked Steve, who sat there listening but not saying anything about the subject. "Have you thought about trying to control someone's reality?" I could tell he didn't want to talk at first. His eyes started roaming between the three of us as he tried to figure out what to say, if he wanted to say anything at all.

"What have you done?" Bobby asked, sensing Steve was thinking hard about our conversation.

"Well …" Steve mumbled. "I wanted my foster parents to get me a car, but they wouldn't."

"So what did you do?" I asked with interest.

He began speaking in a forceful voice. "Since learning how to see into other people's dreams, I've been going into my foster parents' dreams for a while now. I visit them one by one, and sometimes I merge their dreams together. And other times, I bring them to the farmhouse, trying to get them to do what I want them to do." He looked in the distance as he spoke.

"Steve, what did you do to your parents?" Rae asked, worried, as if he was about to tell us something he'd done but shouldn't have.

"After asking them in reality and always hearing 'We'll talk about it later,' or 'We don't want to hear about it anymore' too many times, I decided to take it a step further." He gave us an eerie look.

"But you don't have a car yet. So it didn't work," Bobby surmised.

"Nope. I don't have a car. I have something more important." Steve responded, with more of an upbeat tone in his voice.

"What's that?" I asked.

"Power," he replied, grinning, and he seemed to be looking through our souls.

"You want to elaborate on that?" Rae said.

"Power? We all have powers in our dreams," Bobby reminded Steve.

"No. You don't have the power you believe you have," Steve said, looking at Bobby very seriously.

"Steve, you're worrying me now," Rae said.

"I didn't get the car, because when my foster parents woke from their dreams, we talked about me getting a car. This way, I could verify if it worked or not. And after a few dreams, I started sensing they were becoming scared of me and on the verge of giving me anything I wanted."

"Scared of you?" came Rae's quick reply as we looked at each other with concern.

We sat there for a moment or two but got no response from Steve. "And what did they give you?" I asked again, trying to understand what he was saying.

"I told you. Power." He spoke with authority in his voice.

"So ... how do we do it?" Bobby asked. "There's a fine-looking lady who I want to worship the very ground I walk on."

"I used threats," Steve responded casually.

"*What?*" Rae spoke in a harsh voice to Steve.

"Threats. I scared the hell out of them in dreams until they broke." He chuckled at his accomplishment.

"What the hell are you laughing about?" Rae demanded. "I don't think using threats in reality, let alone dreams, should be used on anyone to get what you want!"

"I didn't hurt them. It was only their dreams," Steve insisted callously. "So why get upset with me when you guys are talking about doing things I've already started doing?"

Steve was right. We wanted what he had accomplished, yet we seemed to be interrogating him for doing it. But if we would have known what else he did—how he treated John—we might not have been willing to follow his lead. Still, I will admit, I was intrigued by the idea.

"That might be the fastest way to try our experiment," I finally spoke up.

Rae questioned my intentions. "Experiment? Come on, David. I don't mind having fun in dreams, and it would be nice to see what would happen in reality, but bullying people to get what we want?"

"Did you try anything else before you used threats?" Bobby asked Steve, trying to get rid of the hostility between us.

"No. I got tired of asking over and over and not getting any-where," Steve responded.

"I think we should give it a try. It would at least let us know if one of us could do what Steve's already done," Bobby said, thinking of Lillie again.

"I still don't understand what you mean by power, though," I told Steve. I wanted a clear answer before I agreed to go along with this.

"It doesn't matter," he said somberly. "I'm just telling you what helped me. It's up to you how you want to try it."

After thinking about it, it really didn't matter if Steve could control someone or not or if any of us could. What mattered was that we were going to try it, regardless if we use threats or a different method. "I'm game. I'd be interested in finding out," I said feeling somewhat excited about trying it. "Rae, what about you?"

"No," she responded. It was the only thing she said.

"You okay?" Bobby asked.

"Yeah, I'm okay. I was just thinking that if we could control a person's reality, then maybe I could help my dad get over my mom's death," she said sorrowfully. "And without using threats!"

"Are you going to try it, then?" Bobby asked her.

"I'm not sure. Part of me wants to find out if I can do it, but part of me would rather not." She sounded concerned about what might happen.

"You seem to be the only one who has actually tried controlling someone's reality. How do we go about it?" I asked Steve.

"I kept telling them in their dreams what I wanted," he explained. "I figured repetition would do it, but it seemed to work just a little. And that's when I started using threats."

"Yeah, shock them into thinking they need to do something when they wake up," Bobby said, as if he already had a plan.

"Shock them?" I questioned with curiosity.

Bobby smiled. "I don't mean to scare the hell out of them, as Steve did, but maybe a little fear might do it. If they don't do it in reality, we keep visiting their dreams, making sure it's the same dream, with a little more scare tactics, until they do it in reality. We keep it up until the change occurs. Or we try something else before we go to that extreme."

"I'm a little worried about giving someone a nightmare," I said.

"You guys do what you want," Rae said suddenly. "It's getting late, and I'm gonna head home."

We didn't agree to do anything, but I guess, after listening to Steve, none of us really needed the other's permission to do anything in our dreams. It was the world we created, but the consequences didn't come into our thought processes as quickly as they should have.

Bobby didn't want to frighten Lillie in her dreams; he just wanted her to feel so comfortable in dreams that reality would take over naturally. So as he lay in his bed, concentrating on Lillie, he soon was at his mansion in his dream. He opened the portal to Lillie's dream and glanced inside.

Hidden in the shadows of the gateway of her dream, Bobby watched Lillie as she and others were in a ski lodge. "Winter? She's dreaming about winter?" Bobby said to himself as he shook his body, acting like he got a cold chill. "Well, if that's what she is dreaming, I guess I need to heat things up." He chuckled and walked through the gateway. Lillie and some of her friends were sitting around the fireplace, and he found a chair next to Lillie.

After making small talk and figuring out a plan, he asked, "You want to dance?"

Lillie looked around at the people standing in winter clothes in the lodge with no music playing. "And where do you think we're going to find a dance floor here?" Lillie asked.

"Oh, baby, I'll take care of the music." Bobby smiled and stretched out his hand toward the fireplace as he kept looking at her.

Lillie saw the fireplace vanish and then everything else in her dream. Now, people were dancing to music while spotlights circled the dance floor, stopping often on a person dancing or sitting and drinking. Couples were in corners, kissing and caressing, while singles were trying to pick someone up at the bar. The music got quieter and softer when Bobby, the DJ, turned the tunes. No longer wearing winter clothes, Lillie walked sensually up to the dance floor in a short dress that fit her like her skin.

Stepping from the turntable, Bobby never took his eyes off of her as she moved her hands across her body to each beat of the song. The crowd cleared path for him as he walked toward Lillie, also moving his body to the rhythm, as multicolored lights filled the area around them. Silently, he stepped close to her, harmonizing his body with hers.

Together they took over the dance floor. Others left when Bobby and Lillie's dance became more erotic, and the world around them gradually dissolved, leaving the two dancing in the middle of heaven itself. As they kissed, stars in the sky soon became twinkles of lights from the candles filling the room, where Bobby and Lillie sat on the floor, stroking each other's faces gently.

Though they were no longer dancing in the heavens or on the dance floor, the flickering flames of the fireplace cast shadow dancers in the room encompassing them. Sipping on wine to quench their thirst, they began trickling wine from the bottle onto each other, cooling the heat that was overwhelming them. Bobby held Lillie as their room slowly vanished, and his bedroom came into view.

Feeling satisfied with what he did in his dream, he used the same dream for a few days. Every time he would look through the threshold of her dreams and see her dreaming of something else, he would change it to the beginning of the dance floor, so she would wake up from him holding her next to the fire. He didn't want to use threats as Steve did. He felt that his charisma was all he needed to get what he wanted.

Rae sat there in the shadow of her dad's dream that separated one side of the table from the other, and which kept Mr. Woods from seeing Rae as she watched him. She wiped her tears in the dimness of the dream, trying to find words to tell her dad. Although she loved him very much, it tore her up, seeing how in the last few years he'd gone from a caring father to someone who just existed in a world of reality that brought only pain.

Her mother's death had been hard on all of them, but Rae resented her dad for not being there to help Mary and her through their sorrow. "Why don't you talk to him?" Mary asked Rae as she appeared on another side of the kitchen table. Rae thought Mary was a part of her dad's dream. "I spend time with Mom most every time I dream," Mary said, and suddenly she was sitting in another chair.

"What?" Rae asked, looking at Mary deeply.

"I visit Mom in my dreams," Mary responded.

"You see me?" Rae asked, as she was still in between her dad's dream and her own.

"Well yeah," Mary responded with a little mockery in her voice.

"Your dreams?" Rae asked, trying to figure out what was happening.

"Yeah, just like you and David, I have learned to control my dreams also," Mary now responded smugly.

Rae woke up, jumped out of bed, and opened Mary's bedroom door. She found Mary sitting up on her bed, smiling. Mary told Rae how she'd heard Rae talking to me one night about dreams, and when she tried it, it worked. She also told Rae how she visited with their mom.

"But why didn't you tell me before now?" Rae asked with astonishment.

"I was spending so much time with Mom and doing other things, I guess I didn't really think about it. Besides, if you couldn't do it, I wasn't going to tell you I could," Mary said, smiling.

"So how did you find me?" Rae asked curiously. "I didn't hear you call my name or sense you were there before I saw you."

"I was going into Dad's dream. I do that now and then, trying to cheer him up and spend time with him," Mary replied. "I bring Dad and Mom together on occasion in his dream. And when I saw you and realized that Dad wasn't aware you were sitting there, I figured you did learn dreams, and I'd let you know I did too."

"But you know it's just a dream, right?" Rae finally spoke.

Mary rolled her eyes at her sister. "Yes. I know it's only a dream."

As they sat there and talked about what Mary had accomplished in dreams, Rae looked at her little sister differently. In fact, she felt that maybe Mary and she had something in common that they could share.

The next morning as we sat in my car parked in her driveway, Rae told me about Mary. "I never thought about dreaming of someone who was dead, let alone my mom."

"Did you try dreaming of your mom?" I asked.

"No, I haven't been to sleep yet. After Mary and I talked some more, I stayed awake, watching her sleep, thinking how happy she must be and seeing Mom in her dreams. But not only that, I was thinking how I was going to approach my dad."

"So you are going to try what we'd talked about, then?"

Rae looked sad. "I'm not sure. If anything, I would like to at least put a bug in my dad's ear to spend a little more time at home, instead of going out." Rae spoke as if she did have a plan. After a few moments of silence, she said, "Since Mary's able to visit his dreams, I'll see if she wants to help. This way, his dreams will be constantly about us." She told me more of her plan and started to feel excited about it. She assured me she wasn't going to use methods that would seem wrong.

Some days later, while eating lunch at a fast-food restaurant, Bobby came in and looked around, as if he was looking for someone. Then he sat down in the booth with Rae and me. "Watch this," he said with enthusiasm. "Shit, man, don't look at me; look behind you," he said quickly. We turned around in time to see Lillie stand up from the table where she was sitting with her friends and walk our way. She stopped at our booth, handed Bobby a note, and walked away.

"Read the note," Rae urged Bobby—he was watching Lillie walk away. "And what are you looking at?" Rae said, slapping my head to get my attention when she saw me watching Lillie also.

"Sorry," I said crouching down in my seat.

Bobby unfolded the note, read it, and said, "I'll be damned." He held the note so we could read it. "Call me" and Lillie's number were the only things on it. It only took Bobby a few days to convince Lillie to make the move on him in reality.

"So? Did you threaten to grab her by her hair to get her to want you?" Rae teased him. "Or did you threaten her family?"

"No, I didn't have to. I just used the gifts of my looks and music. After that, nature took its course," he responded conceitedly.

"Okay," Rae said, but it seemed she couldn't believe him.

The entire time Bobby told us what had happened in his dream, he couldn't stop grinning from ear to ear. "I guess the lady just needed some fine loving," Bobby said, puffing up his body as Rae and I laughed at him.

"But how did you know she was going to be here?" I questioned the coincidence of Lillie's being here and then giving Bobby the note.

"I didn't. But I hoped she would be. After spending time with her in dreams and, just like Steve said, sensing something was about to happen, I notice she started eyeing me more and more. And the rest, as they say, is history." He held up the note.

"Well, we have one more who is able to control dreams," I said.

"Who?" he asked, changing the expression on his face from grin to one of wonder.

Rae told Bobby what she'd told me, bringing him up to speed on what Rae had discovered.

"Mary? Your little sister?" he said incredulously.

"Yep, Mary," she responded excitedly.

"Can anyone do this?" Bobby asked.

"I really don't know," I said. "But I guess I don't want to go around telling people about it too much. If it doesn't work for them, they're going to lock us up in a mental hospital."

"Yeah. I guess we should be careful about who we tell or how we talk about it," Bobby agreed, just before Steve came up.

"What are you grinning about?" Steve asked, sitting down next to Bobby in the booth. Bobby didn't say a word; he just showed him Lillie's name and number on the piece of paper.

"You tried it, then," Steve said, already knowing the answer.

"What about you?" Rae finally asked me.

"No, nothing worked. Or at least, I haven't seen it work yet." I told her, looking around the area to see if I was victorious or not.

"You gonna tell us what you did and with whom?" Bobby questioned.

"I don't want to say just yet. I might jinx it," I responded, and then they all looked at me strangely.

For a few days I kept trying different dreams on my subject. I wasn't sure if it was going to work, because some people just don't want to give in to others; it's all about them. But finally I found out that what I had done actually had worked—it was one day when Rae and I got into the car to leave the school parking lot.

She looked over at Jack's car and questioned the person's identity who was sitting with Jack. "He's with Beth?"

I shrugged. "As Bobby said, it works."

"You had something to do with this?" Rae asked me suspiciously.

"Yep. I sure did," I said rather smugly.

"Who's dream did you go into?" Rae inquired as she looked very hard at me.

"Jackass's," I responded.

"That's more like it. But Beth—why her?" Rae asked.

Jack was one of the most popular kids in school, and I'd set him up with one of the least popular. I really didn't want to tell Rae the truth, but the truth was, I'd spent nights watching Jack dream about Rae, and I couldn't stand it, so I kept ruining Jack's dreams.

Beth wasn't a bad person or even a homely person. She was an average-looking girl who didn't seem to have many boyfriends over the years, if any at all. She was one who would go to the library on a Friday night to do schoolwork. That's what made it hard for me to sway Jack's dream; Beth and Jack were as different as night and day.

"How did you convince him to even talk with her?" Rae asked.

"When I popped into Jack's dream, it always seemed that he dreamed of how wonderful he was and how he could get any woman, including you, that he wanted. And whoever he was dreaming about, I turned into the most hideous person I could think of."

"Hideous?" she asked.

"Yeah. He always had these model-type women in his dreams, and I just wanted him to know that underneath, they might not be what he was expecting." I said, grinning.

"And?"

"And I made the women he was with ugly on the inside, a type of creature."

"So when he dreamed about me? You made me ugly too?"

"I'm taking the fifth on that," I told her, fearing what she might do if I told her the truth of how I made the girls look.

"Bastard," she said and slapped me jokingly. "Just finish the story."

"As I was saying, I would bring Beth into his view and made her almost look like a goddess. And without his knowing that I was speaking to him, I would keep repeating, 'You'd rather be with her'—meaning Beth—'than with one of these women.'"

"And that's all it took?" Rae asked.

"No, believe me, not at all. He kept fighting it. In his dreams, I would show him how his life would turn out with the women he thought he wanted. They would have lots of kids, not having the same sexy body as they did in their younger years, and they'd always be nagging at him. But when it came to Beth, I created the vision of him being waited on, hand and foot. He was able to do anything he wanted to do, and I even had him see Beth negotiate with football teams for him to be able to play. Then I kept watching him at school as he looked her way now and then. But I think the deciding factor was when I put it in his dreams that he would lose millions of dollars by not being able to play sports if he didn't start hanging out with Beth." I felt as my god-like powers had done their best.

"David, that's not right to do that to Beth," Rae said in disappointment.

"I know, but in order for me to believe I could do it, I felt that I had to take opposites and try to bring them together. This way, I know without a doubt it did work. And besides, if I used some-one who he was already hanging out with, how would I know?"

"I understand, but don't you think Beth will be hurt, once he stops paying attention to her?" Rae asked sadly.

I hadn't really thought about that until Rae said it. Hearing it out loud, it felt immoral to use them as test subjects for my own glory in my dreams. I now understood that what I'd done was wrong, and I needed to find a way to break it off between Jack and Beth. But as I thought about it, wouldn't that also hurt Beth? Here was a girl who was having fun, and I was contemplating trying to take it away from her. I didn't care how it would make Jack feel, but God knows I wasn't trying to hurt Beth. I changed the subject abruptly. And now, I truly understood what Steve meant when he said "power."

"Have you been able to talk with your dad yet?" I asked Rae.

"No, every time I go into his dreams to put a thought in his mind, I just sit there," she replied in a low voice. Then she became excited. "But I have been spending time with Mary and my mom."

"Oh, yeah? How do you feel about having a dream about your mom?"

"I agree with Mary. I know our mom is dead. But if we can spend time with her in dreams, I'll take dreaming of someone I love and want to be with any day over waking up from a dream I have no control over that doesn't make sense to me."

"I agree," I told her as I started thinking how my dreams seemed to be better also.

When I asked about Mary, Rae told me she was doing okay. "Her dream world consists of the family being together most of the time. She even told me once that she'd rather stay sleeping and enjoying life as it should have been, instead of waking up to how it is."

I thought about what Rae just said and wondered if maybe we were in our dreams too much. Maybe they were starting to control us, instead of us controlling them.

"So where's lover-boy and Steve?" Rae asked me.

"I think Bobby is out with Lillie. And Steve, I haven't seen him since the day he came into the restaurant," I answered. "When

Lillie gave Bobby her number. So I'm not sure what's going on with him."

"I saw him the day before yesterday," Rae said, seeming concerned. "He was with a couple of other kids in a car. When I waved at him, he acted like he didn't know me."

"Really? I wonder what's going on with that?" I realized then that Steve had been staying away from us more and more. I pulled up to Rae's house to drop her off.

"I'm going to take my car to school tomorrow," she told me as we sat in the driveway.

"Okay, but why? I can pick you up in the morning."

She smiled. "I'm picking up Mary after school. We're going to go out and do sister stuff for the night. Dreams are nice, but I want to spend more time with her in reality also."

After leaving Rae, I drove home, thinking about Steve again and how he was distant from the group. When we, as a group, wanted to hang out together in dream world, Steve wanted to be by himself. At first it was just in dreams, but now, it started to be in reality also. Now and then we would get together, or he'd come up to us, but after he found out what we'd been doing, he would disappear for a few days and often missed school too.

Throughout our experience in dream world, each of us had mastered one gift over another. Just as the rest of us did, Mary learned the ability to use time alteration as a way of keeping her dreams going as long as possible. When she sensed she was waking up, she'd learned to stay in her dreams until the last possible moment. The reason she chose this over any other ability was to spend more time with her mom.

Rae used her gifts to create different dream worlds within the same dream. As her dream progressed, if she didn't like the scenery, she would change the layout. She told us that there was always something better, and unless we tried different views, we weren't going to find what we really were looking for. I personally think it was more of her trying to find the right way to talk to her dad. But that's okay; she was doing it her way.

What can I say about Bobby? He didn't need to keep a dream longer or change the landscape of a dream to enjoy it. The gift he used the most was what he called the dream wish. Every time we'd meet in dream world, he always had something new—a different car, house, clothes, or even planes to take him all around his dream world. Since he couldn't live the exciting life in reality, he said he was going to live it in dreams. Bobby had indeed become the playboy of dream world.

I was like everyone else. We were able to use the gifts each of us had; we just used the one we preferred the most. Like flying, for instance. I like to fly in my dreams. Not in a plane, as Bobby did, but as birds fly. And since I used that the most, that was my strongest gift. My flying consisted of me just standing on the ground one second, and the next, I was floating in the air. Once I did that, I could think of any place I wanted to go, and I was headed in that direction, passing through portals as I searched for what I wanted to do.

Steve was no different than any of us with using his dream gifts. Just like us, he used his gifts to his advantage. But none of us cared for his gift too much, as we soon learned: Over time, we realized some things in reality shouldn't be changed. Steve wasn't concerned about flying, changing the landscape, or whatever; he wanted the power to control his reality and his dreams. And he was now willing to do anything to get it.

Steve was the one who had shared with us the ability to affect reality by using dreams. He had become the master of it, and his only concern was to change the reality around him. This way, he had the best of both worlds. What he was doing that we weren't aware of at the time was changing a lot of people's realities. And not only did our reality change on that night Steve was picked up by the cops for a stolen car, but our dreams had changed too.

CHAPTER 5 LOST IN DREAMS

The old lady stood in the middle of the desert, feeling the heat upon her aged body as the midday sun's rays turned her light complexion red and dried her wrinkling skin. As she fell down on her hands and knees on the hot grains of sand, she could see the life-saving creek as it ran through the desert hills, only a few yards from where she sat begging for water.

As she crawled those last yards of her life, the sweat droplets from her face and neck fell as raindrops, only to evaporate into a mist before hitting the ground. She was willing to give everything she had, including her soul, for some water to cool her dry, hot throat. "Please help me," she said, struggling to say the words as she pleaded to the silhouette on the other side of the creek.

With a cold and callous heart, he shouted unmercifully back at her. "What do you want from me?" His voice rang out, piercing the woman's ears, as shockwaves from his body knocked her backward farther from the water in the desert.

"I want water," the woman mumbled in agony. The grains of sand tore into her knees and arms as she tried desperately to crawl back toward the creek once more.

Without sympathy or remorse for what he had done, he called to her, "I want something too!"

"Please help me," she begged again, giving all of her strength to the words that were barely heard as she fell face first into the sand.

"What do you need from me?" the loathsome voice spoke as his silhouette bent over and took a drink of the cool water from the creek.

"I need water," she whispered.

The outline of a man floated over the creek and landed a few feet from where she lay crying. "I need something too," came his dispassionate response. He sat the woman up, and the scene changed from sand and heat in the desert to snow and cold winds blowing across barren fields.

He stood on the outside of the snowstorm and watched the woman sitting in the snow, shivering from the winds that passed through her body. "Why do you continue to ignore my request?" he questioned the tired woman.

"Please stop," she pleaded, holding herself to stay warm. Her tears formed into ice crystals that fell in the snow.

"Then give me what I want," he demanded in an angry voice as he walked into the blizzard, wearing an oversized coat.

"I'm begging you—please get me out of here." Her body shuddered uncontrollable when he stopped in front of her.

"You always want from me, but you don't give in return," he whispered into her ear. Now they stood in a grassy field, surrounded by fire that danced all around them and was moving closer.

"Anything! Anything!" the woman screamed in desperation as he let her feel the heat of the flames.

"In here, I control life." The voice rang out from some-where on the other side of the flames that had started to overwhelm her.

"Stop! You can have it! Please stop it!" The woman's voice shrieked over and over in anguish as she begged for deliverance as the flames started reaching her ... and she woke up, out of breath, shivering, and covered in sweat. The woman looked around her bedroom and then broke down crying from the nightmare Steve had just given her.

Steve had become so obsessed with wanting what he didn't have in reality that he spent time learning how to manipulate the dreams of others to get what he wanted. But it was more than that—he also got very skilled at frightening people to the point that when they'd meet him in reality, they were very concerned about their welfare and were willing to do anything to get rid of him. After frightening the old lady to the point of death in her dreams many times, Steve now stood outside her home once again, waiting for her to come out the door.

She was reluctant to hand over her late husband's prize, but seeing Steve standing at the end of her driveway, and remembering his face from the nightmares, she seemed to be hypnotized. And although she had refused to do it the last few mornings when she saw him, she now went back into the house and returned with the keys to a mint-condition, white-with-red-interior, '64 Mustang that Steve had been infatuated with.

Even though we had the capability of control people's reality through their dreams, it took time for most people to listen to their dreams and do something in reality, especially if it was something they didn't want to do. But instead of giving it time to take root in the woman's consciousness, Steve hurried the process, and that didn't give it time to have a permanent effect. Once Steve drove off with her car, she came to her senses and called the police, saying a teenager had just stolen her car. And later that night, the police picked up Steve.

"I already told you. I didn't steal the car; she gave it to me," Steve told the detective as he sat in the interrogation room later that evening.

"Yeah, I know. You dreamed it up and there it was," Detective Mike Long replied, looking at Steve with disbelief.

"No, I said I was able to control her by using her dreams. That's how I got the car. How many times do I have to tell you that? The lady gave it to me!"

"If she gave it to you, why did she call us to say it was stolen?" the detective inquired as he sat on the opposite side of the table.

"I already told you," Steve said one more time.

"Look, son, we can do the insanity plea if you want. I have a friend who works at Lifelong Institution, and I'm more than happy to call him. But do you really want to go down that road?" Detective Long said, trying to scare Steve into talking.

Tears formed in Steve's eyes as he tried to hide his emotion from the officer, and Detective Long recognized his advantage and continued explaining to Steve how much trouble he was in. "But right now you're looking at a felony for a stolen vehicle. That will get you time in jail. Which would you rather have? Time in jail or a stay in the institution?" When Steve didn't say anything, the detective gave Steve one more thing to think about. "In addition to the charge of stealing the car, you're facing possible money-laundering charges. Seventeen-year-old boys don't drive around with over fifty thousand dollars in a stolen vehicle. You could be looking at over twenty years in prison," the detective said, now sealing Steve's fate.

Wiping tears from his eyes, Steve looked up at Detective Long. "I didn't steal the car."

"Where did the money come from?" Detective Long asked.

Steve was now sobbing uncontrollably and unable to speak.

"You know, I don't believe you stole the car for yourself. And I don't think the money is yours. If you're covering up for someone, now would be a good time to let me know. There's no reason for you to go to prison or even an institution for someone else," the detective said in a more compassionate voice.

"But okay, he said after a pause, "let's go with your dream story. How did you learn to control dreams?"

Steve took a drink of water to get control himself. "I didn't. A friend of mine was the one who told me how to do it."

"Who's this friend of yours?" Detective Long asked.

"Does it matter? You don't believe me; why would you believe him?"

The detective shuffled some papers around the table, momentarily ignoring Steve's question. Then he said, "Well, sometimes we just need the other person to corroborate a story. Wouldn't you want us to work together so I can believe you?"

"I don't know," Steve whined. "I just want to sleep right now. Can't I go?"

"No, son, you can't go home. If anything, you'll be spending the night in a cell here. You'll be charged with a stolen vehicle and money laundering," Detective Long said, smiling at Steve as if he enjoyed telling him that. "I can be here all night. And I have no problem keeping you awake, asking questions. If you're tired and want to sleep, you need to tell us what's going on."

Steve started rubbing his hands together, trying to dry his sweating palms. "David told us."

"Who?" Detective Long looked up from his paperwork to stare at Steve.

"David. David was the one who told us about controlling dreams and how we can influence others inside them," Steve said with conviction.

"David who?" the detective asked. He listened intently and made notes on a piece of paper as Steve explained what we could do.

"And that's how I was able to get the lady's car," Steve said, finishing the story. "I didn't steal it."

Detective Long now had all information he needed about Rae, Bobby, and me. And then he got angry at Steve. "Even if you didn't steal the car, I should lock your ass up for harassment and threats!" The detective spoke, loathing Steve for how he had treated the woman, even though it was in a dream.

He left the room, telling the officer sitting outside the door to take Steve back to the holding cell. Detective Long's partner, Detective Yoder, had been watching the interrogation from the observation room. When Detective Long joined his partner, Detective Yoder said, "Mike, I really believe you need to call Jerry over at Lifelong." Detective Long stood there in silence for a moment, and Detective Yoder continued talking. "This kid believes he has the power to control dreams and even control people's reality by using their dreams against them."

"Yeah, I was thinking about that. His mind is out there. And the drug test came back only showing small traces of pot, nothing else," Detective Long said after looking at a report he held in his hands.

"And what about his friends? He thinks they can do the same thing. You really aren't going to check this story out, are you?" Dale Yoder asked.

"No, I don't believe his story. But I do want to check out his friends. These kids are into something, and I want to find out what it is. And whatever they're doing, maybe we can get the person who is in charge." Detective Long looked at his partner with uncertainty. "What do you think?"

"I think he's a nutcase, and you need to get hold of Jerry Maiden," Dale responded, tapping the file in Mike's hand.

"I believe he is aware of his dreams, and even understands he's dreaming. There's nothing wrong with that. I myself am a lucid dreamer. In my dreams I'm conscious of what I'm doing."

"Being aware of you're dreaming is one thing, but saying you can control them or even others is a case for the hospitals, as far as I'm concerned," Dale said strongly.

Mike Long looked at his paperwork and the recorder in his hand. "I agree that he does need help. I'm going to get him over to Lifelong tonight so Jerry can talk with him first thing in the morning."

"You want me to pick up his friends?" Yoder asked as he opened the door to leave.

"No, we can wait on the paperwork for them in the morning. Besides, we can talk to all three of them at one time if we go to their school first thing. And since they don't know we have their friend, they're not going to be expecting anything," Detective Long said, following Detective Yoder down the hall and into their office.

But the detectives weren't right about everything. Even though we weren't sure what was going on, Steve had appeared inside my dream as I stood on the pier at the pond, fishing.

"David." I heard Steve's voice behind me.

"Where have you been?" I questioned, looking at him when he walked through the portal of his dream into mine after we made contact. "Steve?" I watched him just standing there, not saying anything but looking as if he wanted to tell me something. Setting my pole down, I walked to the end of the pier next to him. "Hey, you okay?"

"I told the cops about us," he whispered.

"What do you mean, you told the cops about us?"

"Our ability to control dreams, I told—"

"Steve? Steve!" I raised my voice louder as I called his name, thinking I could talk with him after he abruptly left my dream. But I stood there alone at the pond and thought about what it meant that Steve had shared our secrets. Looking around at the pond and trees, I saw them dissolving as I woke myself up.

"Okay, son, you can't sleep just yet," the detective said, waking Steve up after he had dozed off in his cell. Feeling unsteady and looking around in his cell, Steve whispered, "I hope you understood."

"What are you mumbling about?" Detective Long asked. Steve looked away without saying anything. Long handcuffed Steve and led him out of the cell. "Very well."

"I got the papers," Detective Yoder said as he came up alongside of Long and Steve as they walked down the hall of the police station. He handed Mike a judge's order for Steve's seventy-two-hour commitment at Lifelong.

"We're going to take you to talk to a friend of ours," Detective Long said after reading the papers.

"Who?" Steve inquired.

"Jerry Maiden," the detective told Steve as they headed out the doors of the police station.

"Who's that, and why do I need to talk to him?" Steve said, trying to get himself under control.

"He's a friend of mine and one of the leading doctors at Lifelong."

"Lifelong?" Steve was scared now as he heard where he was going. "You don't believe me, do you?" Steve started struggling to get away from both Long and Yoder, who held onto his arms as they tried putting him in the car.

"Steve, stop fighting. It's not going to get you anywhere. And it doesn't matter if I believe you or not. You need help," Detective Long spoke, trying to calm Steve down.

"At least let me call my parents," he said, still struggling with the handcuffs as he sat in the backseat of the car.

"We've already called your foster parents. They said it was in your best interest to get help. And as soon as the doctors at the institute allow it, they will come to visit," Detective Yoder said in a somewhat cold manner.

Steve sat there staring out the window when he heard how his foster parents reacted.

His foster parents wouldn't even get a lawyer to find out about the legal ramifications of his situation. They just took the word of the detectives, not questioning it or even being willing to see him before he was confined. "That's nothing new," he said in a low voice, feeling abandoned by the very ones who said they would watch over him as parents. It seemed that these foster parents weren't any different than all the others he'd had throughout his life.

Not all foster parents were as uncaring as Steve's were, but his luck with foster care went from bad to worse as he was passed from family to family, until he ended up with the Kennedys. And the Kennedys only wanted the money the state was giving them to take care of Steve and the other children in their care. They didn't give a damn about the kids they were supposed to take care of, and it showed by their unwillingness to help Steve in his time of trouble.

When they reached Lifelong, Steve became more up-set and fought the detectives as they practically lugged him into the institution. Orderlies came to their aid and dragged Steve down the hall into a small room. Steve kicked, fought, screamed and cussed, until a doctor arrived to inject a seda-tive into Steve's arm. It calmed him down and eventually put him to sleep.

As Steve was being taken to Lifelong, I sat in my bedroom thinking how he disappeared from my dream. What had he meant by his comment about telling the cops what we were ca-pable of doing? About an hour later, I went back to sleep with the intention of trying to find Steve in his dreams. I called his name in dream world but couldn't contact him, so I went back to the pond, hoping he had returned there.

Not seeing him at the pond, I started calling Rae's name in the air, hoping she was asleep and able to hear me. "Rae," I spoke again after not getting a response the first time.

"Hi, David." I heard her voice carrying in the wind.

"We need to talk," I told her as she slowly faded into view; she stood in front of me, with her own dream in the background on the other side of the dream door.

"What's up?" Rae questioned as she stepped through the door that separated her dream from my own, leaving the door open to where I could see part of her dream. She saw me staring through the gateway and asked, "What do you think?"

"I never took you for someone who was into the solar systems," I responded in awe. I saw worlds of many colors in the foreground of a dark universe, filled with flashing lights of stars through the night skies.

In addition, I saw different colored clouds drifting around some of the planets, while rainbows of light encompassed other worlds. They seemed to dance from world to world.

"I enjoy creating these," she said, smiling as she too looked past the door into her dream. And then, the door vanished as Rae passed her hand in front of it.

"So, what's up?" she asked again, giving me a kiss hello on the cheek.

"Have you heard from Steve?" I questioned, getting to the point as we walked around the pond and headed into the woods.

"No. I haven't seen him for some time," she said, seeming unconcerned.

We walked along the path in the woods, watching the animals, which would be wild in reality but came to our summons in dreams. I declined to tell her what Steve told me so that she wouldn't be worried over something I wasn't sure of yet. After enjoying our dream together, we said good-bye, and she faded from my arms as we kissed one more time, leaving me to search for Steve.

Unable to find Steve anywhere in dream world where I was searching, I thought about his farmhouse that I visited a few times in other dreams. Waving my hand to open a portal to his house and stepping through, I started looking at his world. The only things around were trees, farming equipment, and fields that looked as if someone was farming them. I knew Steve was somewhat of a loner, but with Rae, Bobby, and me as friends, he never had to feel alone, especially in dream world, where we could make anything happen.

Unlike Bobby's mansions, Steve's house looked like any house one would find in reality. It was a two-story, simple farmhouse, grayish, with white trim on the windows and doors. The porch had a white railing that wrapped completely around the house, and chairs and small tables followed its path.

Walking up the steps of the porch, I could see the front door was open, and I peered through the screen door. I knocked but got no answer, so I opened the screen door and poked my head in, calling for Steve. Still not getting a response, I walked down the small hall to the living room.

The light from outside was fading as I went farther into the room, but I saw candle sconces lining the walls. I spoke a few words, and shadows started flickering around objects as the flames from the candles grew brighter. There were pictures of men, women, and couples also hanging on the walls. One of the photos was of Steve's current foster parents; my assumption was the others might also have been foster parents at one time or another.

As I continued looking around and calling Steve's name, I noticed another couple's picture. I didn't know them personally, but had seen a picture of them on the news. And as I recollected, they were taken to a mental hospital because of a nervous breakdown—something about someone stalking them and doing cruel acts to them. I never did hear the entire story, but I do remember they said it was in their nightmares that something told them to hurt each other, so the dreams would stop. I didn't think about it then, but now I wondered if Steve had something to do with it.

And then I saw a picture of Sue, his sister. Her portrait was hanging above the fireplace with candles surrounding it. When I waved my hand across them, they lit up, revealing a shrine around the portrait. As I continued to see more and more pictures around the room, I began to believe that Steve was using these photos to contact people in their dreams. I left the house and started looking around outside.

"David." I heard Bobby's voice calling me.

"Yeah, Bobby." I looked around to see the portal that would connect us. Standing in front of the house, I felt the wind starting to blow around me and then form into a circle that was bluish in color and then mixing with green, creating the door between our dreams.

"I've been calling you for some time now," Bobby said from the other side.

"Really?" I thought that was odd since I was in a dream and should have heard him. "I just now heard you."

As the portal started to become clearer, I could see Bobby in a swimming pool with a drink in his hand and girls in bikinis on floats around him. "Did you forget?" he said, chuckling. He moved his hand around in order to move the portal to his dream for me to see more of the party he was throwing in dream world.

"Where's Lillie?" I asked disapprovingly.

"I had to let her go. It was almost like I forced myself on her in dreams. I didn't feel right doing that. So, these dreamers are here to have fun and nothing more." He grinned. "Are you coming or not?"

"No, I decided to go fishing instead." I knew that if I went to Bobby's dream party, it wouldn't go too well with Rae.

"Where are you?" Bobby asked as he saw Steve's house behind me. "Is that Steve's place?"

"Yes. Have you seen him?"

"No, I haven't. But when you do see him, let him know that

a nice paint job would make a world of difference," Bobby said, chuckling.

"Okay, I sure will. Thanks. See you in reality." I broke contact with Bobby's dream. After watching the gateway to Bobby's world dissolve, I lifted myself up and floated around the countryside, hoping I might see Steve somewhere, until I heard my alarm clock, reminding me of the reality I needed to get back to.

"Were you able to find Steve?" Rae asked after I picked her up for school.

"No, did he get in contact with you in your dreams?" I asked hopefully.

"No, Mary and I spent the rest of our dreams finishing up some of the new worlds we created. She's getting pretty good at dream world. In fact, she's able to conjure up all kinds of things. And the powers she's acquiring are beyond what we've been doing," Rae said, smiling at her sister's gift.

Then she looked at me. "Is something wrong?"

I shook my head. "I'm not sure. The reason I contacted you was because Steve contacted me. But as fast as he came into my dream, he was gone. I don't know what to think." I told her, as I still felt uneasy about the whole thing.

"Maybe he found something else to do and decided not to bother you," she suggested, trying to assure me everything was fine.

"Maybe," I replied quietly, although I didn't believe it to be true.

Later, when all three of us were together at our normal lunch table, we could talk in private. "I tried to contact him," I explained, "but looking around his house, it was kind of weird, seeing all the pictures, and then seeing Sue's portrait hanging above the mantel as if she was being worshipped or something."

"You think he was trying to tell us that he told the cops what we can do?" Rae asked fearfully.

"Nope, he definitely did," Bobby said as he pointed in the direction of two gentlemen in suits with the assistant principal coming into the cafeteria and walking our direction.

"Shit." The word came out of my mouth in disbelief.

"Well, I'm not telling anyone what I can do," Bobby insisted. "They'll lock my ass up and throw away the key. You know damn well they will." Bobby became more nervous as the men came closer.

"Then we need to play it off, if that's the case," Rae said, agreeing with Bobby.

Mr. Douglas, the assistant principal, and the two men stopped next to the table where we were eating our lunch. "This is Detective Long and Detective Yoder," Mr. Douglas said. "They would like to ask you some questions."

"Mr. Douglas, is everything okay?" Rae asked, sounding concerned.

Before he could answer, Detective Yoder asked, "Is there somewhere we can talk in private?"

"Sure, follow me," Mr. Douglas replied and led us all through a side door, heading to a small conference room. After Mr. Douglas left us, Rae, Bobby, and I started feeling more nervous.

"I'd like to ask you a couple of questions regarding Steve Holcomb," Detective Mike Long said.

"Is Steve okay? Nothing happened to him, did it?" Rae spoke up first, trying to hide the tension in her voice.

"He's fine," Long said. "We just need to ask a couple of questions."

"Sure," I said, trying to hide my fear.

"How well do you know Steve?" Detective Long asked.

"We've known him for about three years," I answered for all of us, while looking at Bobby and Rae.

"He's a good friend of ours," Bobby said, trying to maintain his composure.

"Is Steve in trouble?" Rae asked.

"Let me ask the questions for now," the detective told us. "Does he have a car?"

"Car?" Bobby said quickly. "Man, we chauffeur him around."

"So, he didn't have a car?" the detective confirmed.

"No, Bobby's right," Rae responded. "Any time he needed to go somewhere, one of us would have to take him."

"Shit, the only way that dude is getting a car is if he stole it because his tight-ass foster parents aren't going to buy him one," Bobby spoke more confidently to the detectives.

"He stole a car, didn't he?" Rae asked, certain that she was right. "Are you kidding me?"

"Oh, man." Bobby spoke with disbelief.

"One more question," Detective Long said. "Has he said anything about dreams to you?"

Here it was. The question we were all concerned about that put us on the spot and eventually might put us in an institution if we said the wrong thing. We were sure of only one thing: Steve had told. Rae sat there in a daze, Bobby was no longer laughing as he tried to look seriously into the detective's eyes, and I was frightened. I couldn't look at Detective Long or Yoder, as I tried to act as if I was pondering the question.

"Dreams?" Rae tried to look perplexed by such a question.

"Yes, dreams. Are you able to control your dreams?" Detective Yoder now asked.

"Control dreams?" I inquired sounding dumbfounded.

"I have some pretty good ones I would like to repeat," Bobby spoke up, chuckling again, trying to relax.

"Detective, what's going on?" Rae asked. "Steve is our friend. We don't know anything about him and a car or the dreams that you're referring to, but he is our friend, and we would like to know if he's okay."

"Well, you don't have to worry about him. He's being taken care of. And I'm sure his foster parents would tell you anything if they felt you needed to know," Detective Long said.

"Is he in jail?" I asked.

"Two months left, huh?" Detective Long said, ignoring my question.

"Excuse me?" I tried to understand what he meant.

"Before graduation. Two months, correct?" he replied.

"Yes, but what's that have to do with Steve?" Rae asked.

"Nothing. I just wanted to say congratulations." He stood up and smiled. "And if there's anything else I can think of, I'm sure we will be talking again." He left the room with Yoder.

We looked at each other without saying a word as we sat in the conference room. Hearing the end-of-lunch bell, we left the room and headed toward our next class. "Now what are we going to do?" Bobby asked with concern. Before Rae or I could answer, Lillie walked up, told Bobby she would like to see him again, and walked away.

"Maybe we shouldn't have tried to control others using their dreams against them," I said regretfully as I watched Lillie walk away from us.

"I haven't messed with her dreams in a while," Bobby assured us. "I only used Lillie's dreams to get her to notice me at the beginning and nothing else. Besides, I'm not the twisted one." Bobby shook his head in defense of what he'd done to Lillie.

"Where do you think Steve is?" Rae asked sadly.

"I would say one of two places: jail or the mental ward," I responded.

"And if we tell the cops he's telling the truth about what we are able to do, that's exactly where we all are going to end up, if not some research facility," Bobby said, sounding upset.

While the two detectives had been interrogating us, the head doctor at Lifelong, Jerry Maiden, was also questioning Steve.

"Please calm down and sit, or I'll have you sedated again," Dr. Maiden said in a demanding voice.

"The hell with you. I'm telling you the truth!" Steve bellowed over and over, trying to get someone to believe him. "You have no right to keep me here!" He paced around the room as best as he could while wearing ankle cuffs and handcuffs.

"Mr. Holcomb, we have three days to determine if a judge will decide to keep you here longer or not. And if you continue acting this way, I assure you I will let the judge know you need confinement. But it's up to you how you want to handle this. Now, do as I told you and sit down so we can resolve this issue."

"Yeah, whatever," Steve replied, rolling his eyes and sitting in the chair.

"Now, as I understand it, you were picked up in a stolen car with a large amount of money. Is that true?" Dr. Maiden asked.

"You have the report," Steve snarled.

"Yes, I already knew the answer, but I'm trying to get you to relax and talk," Maiden responded.

"Relax? How the hell can anyone relax in a nut ward?" Steve said as he started laughing.

"Mr. Holcomb, please let's get back to your issue. And when the detectives asked you about it, you said you were able to control your dreams. And I might add, you said you could control people's realities by using their own dreams against them. And that's how you got the car and money. Is that correct?"

Feeling nervous, Steve stood up again, only to hear Maiden tell him to sit back down or he would call an orderly to put him back in the chair.

"Piss off!" Steve shot at him.

"Don't test me," Maiden said, clicking his pen in his hand. "It will go a lot easier for you if you cooperate." Dr. Maiden tried speaking compassionately.

Steve still was unruly, but he didn't want the orderlies in the room, so he decided to stay seated.

"Why do you think you can control dreams and others?"

Understanding he was running out of options quickly, Steve decided to say anything the doctor wanted to hear.

"Fine, yes, I stole the car, and the money was from another car I had stolen. I'm a car runner." Steve hoped he sounded convincing.

"A car runner?" Maiden questioned, raising an eyebrow.

"Yes. I steal a car and people pay me. There you have it. Now can I leave?" Steve said, trying very much to find a way out of Lifelong.

"Well, that will help the police put their pieces together. But according to Detective Long, you believe you have the ability to control dreams. That's where I come in," the doctor said.

"You son of a bitch. I told you what you wanted to hear. I admitted I stole the car and got money for it, and now your ass wants to keep me in this damn nut house!" Steve said furiously and tried his best to throw things around the room.

After calling for an orderly, two men came into the room. One gave Dr. Maiden a syringe and helped the other orderly subdue Steve. Steve struggled to get loose before he was injected. "Don't do this. I told you the truth. Please, don't."

"Mr. Holcomb, stop this!" Maiden responded.

"I can't contact my friends in their dreams if you do this!" Steve cried out as tears started forming in his eyes.

"I'm sorry. But from your own mouth you just said, 'I can't contact my friends in their dreams.' You need help, and this is the only way I can help you." Maiden stuck the needle in Steve's arm.

After a few moments, Steve was feeling lightheaded and dizzy. "I'm telling the truth. I can control ..." he said, just as he passed out.

"We'll talk tomorrow, Mr. Holcomb," Jerry Maiden said, knowing Steve couldn't hear him.

"You have your hands full with this one," one of the orderlies said, as he and his coworker put Steve in a wheelchair and headed out the door.

"Will you ask Mrs. Kalien to come into my office?" Dr. Maiden spoke to the orderlies. He took a deep breath to calm himself down and walked over to the window. "Did they really get this far?" he asked himself.

"Excuse me, sir?" his secretary, Mrs. Kalien, said as she came into the office.

"Please contact a Colonel Donald Tillian. His number is in my address book," he said, "and arrange a meeting between us." Then he went back to staring out the window, thinking of a project years ago.

CHAPTER 6 DREAM PATROL

We did have a couple of months to go before graduation. And instead of getting excited about leaving high school forever, as the rest of the kids were doing, we spent our time trying to figure out what had happened to Steve and what might become of us if Detective Long believed we too were able to control dreams. Even though Long didn't tell us Steve had stolen a car, we felt confident Steve was in jail for some reason.

When we went to Steve's house, his foster parents told us he was being taken care of and we shouldn't worry. Then we went to the police station, hoping we could see him, if he was there at all, but we were only told they couldn't give out any information. For a couple days, we tried to contact him through dreams but weren't able to, except for one night when I heard him call my name. I couldn't maintain contact with him, however, so our only hope was that he was, in fact, being taken care of.

"Jerry!" Donald Tillian said as Mrs. Kalien showed him into Dr. Maiden's office. "It's good to see you." He reached out to shake Jerry's hand.

"Colonel, nice to see you, too," Maiden said.

"Three years has been too long. And I'm retired now," Colonel Tillian spoke with a chuckle, "but still working on projects for the military."

"Sit down, Colonel. Would you like some brandy?"

"No, too early for me," Tillian responded with a smile. "So ... what's on your mind?" he asked, wondering why his long-ago friend would have sent for him.

"Still getting to the point, I see," Maiden replied.

"Well, if you want to come back, I'm sure I can use you on one of the projects I'm working on," Tillian said, as if that's what Dr. Maiden wanted.

"No, I'm very content here," Jerry said and then poured himself a glass of brandy. "I find it's a lot easier to deal with kids on this side of the line."

"Okay, Jerry, it's great to see you too, but you seem to have something on your mind. So why am I here?"

The doctor lifted the bottle of brandy toward the colonel, offering him a drink once more. When the colonel refused again, Maiden took the last gulp of brandy in his glass and then said, "Are you still working on Dream Catcher?"

Tillman looked very critically at Dr. Maiden. "What's this all about?" Tillian asked sharply. He wanted his own question answered when he heard the phrase "Dream Catcher."

"Please, Don, answer my question first," Dr. Maiden said adamantly.

"You know I can't tell you that," Tillian said, feeling a little uneasy about the conversation.

"Yes, I know. But I need to know if you are working on Dream Catcher or not." Tillian hesitated, thinking about how he was going to answer. "Are you?" Maiden asked one more time, raising his voice.

"Jerry, we've been friends for a very long time. You and I both worked on that project. If there's something going on, I need to know," Colonel Tillian said and then walked over to stand right next to Dr. Maiden.

"I didn't work on the project, other than trying to piece together the brains of those kids, whatever they had left after you did your experiments on them," Jerry said, getting upset as he remembered.

"Did you call me here just to argue about the past?" Tillian spoke severely.

"No, I didn't. I just want to find out if the project is still going on."

Both men stood there in silence thinking about the test they'd performed for a project called Dream Catcher. Colonel Tillian finally told Maiden that he was no longer on the project.

"That's too bad," Jerry said.

"Too bad?" Tillian asked, surprised.

"Yes, I think we found one of the subjects a few days ago," Jerry said.

Tillian seemed concerned by Maiden's response and the expression on his face. "What do you mean, you found one of the subjects?" Tillian asked.

"A few days ago, a detective friend of mine brought a kid to me, Steve Holcomb. He was picked up for stealing a car, and they even found a good deal of money in the vehicle. When the detective questioned him, he kept saying he was able to control dreams—his own dreams and other people's."

"What makes you believe he might have been a part of Dream Catcher or even that he has the abilities?" Tillian spoke with curiosity.

"After listening to the kid's story, I was curious if he was one of your subjects that somehow got loose," Jerry explained. "I ran scans and tests, similar to what we did on the project. Don, the kid's brainwaves were not only identical to the brainwaves of the kids in the experiments but also many times stronger than what I came across."

Colonel Tillian took a deep breath and let it out slowly as he walked toward Maiden's office bar. "I'll have that drink now," he said as he tried to get his thoughts together. "What about the tests? How were you able to determine his abilities?" Tillian asked, finishing his drink in one swallow.

"Since he's been here, I've had to keep him sedated because of his outbursts of violence and, naturally, because of my concern for him. I wanted to know if I had to put his mind back together, so I let the drugs wear off to monitor his sleep. When he reached the dream state, his brain went into overdrive, and then I heard him calling for someone by the name of David in his sleep. I believe he was making dream contact. Then I increased the medicine to keep him from focusing in his dream," Maiden said, finishing his story.

"Hell, Jerry, my grandson speaks in his sleep," Tillian chuckled.

"Don, you know damn well we wouldn't be sitting here having this conversation if I didn't believe it. Why do you think you're here, especially if it has anything to do with Dream Catcher?" Maiden responded harshly.

"Fair enough," the colonel finally said. He finished the drink Jerry just poured for him. "Dream Catcher was shut down a few years ago. We couldn't get the test subjects to control their dreams, let alone someone else's," Tillian explained.

"Well, someone apparently has learned it," Jerry said confidently.

"What about this David kid he called for? Does he have the abilities?" Tillian said, now getting more interested.

"I'm not sure. When I first talked to the boy, he started getting physical, so I had to sedate him. But just before he passed out, he said, 'Don't put me under. I can't contact my friends in their dreams if you do.'"

"Where's the kid at now?" the colonel asked.

"We're still keeping him sedated," Maiden responded.

"Who else knows about this?" Colonel Tillian asked.

"No one, other than the detectives who brought him in the other night, as far as I know," Maiden said. "Oh, and the judge who signed the order to keep Holcomb here longer than the three days upon my request."

"Your request?" Tillman asked. "Why request the longer stay?"

"I felt the kid was delusional, but I wanted extra time to run my own test," Maiden replied.

"Okay, where do I come in? What do you want me to do with him?" the colonel asked, knowing already what he was going to do.

"I don't know ... I just don't know. I really believe he has the ability to do what he says he does, after our work on Dream Catcher. But how can we keep him drugged up all the time?" Dr. Maiden asked rhetorically.

"You know I'm going to take him back with me," Tillian told Maiden, not giving him a choice in the matter.

"Yes, I know," Jerry said in a low voice.

"If you knew I was going to take him, why did you call me?" Tillian questioned.

"I didn't have any other choice. I can't leave him here, and I can't leave him out in public either," Dr. Maiden replied disappointedly.

"I'll get the paperwork started, and we can transfer him to another facility tonight," Tillian said. "Also, I need to find out who this David kid is. You said a detective friend of yours brought him in. Would he know where I could find David?"

Tillian left Dr. Maiden's office to start the transfer process to take Steve into custody. He visited Detective Long the next morning.

"Captain?" Detective Long said when his captain came in the office with Tillian.

"Mike, this is retired Colonel Tillian. He has some questions he'd like to ask you," the captain told the detective with a disturbed look on his face.

"So what can I help you with, Colonel?" Mike asked.

"If you have a minute, I'd like to talk to you about a young boy you took to Lifelong the other night, a Steve Holcomb," Tillian said.

"Colonel, tell me this: why is the military concerned with a routine felony charge of a stolen vehicle?" Detective Long inquired, wasting no time.

"Mike ..." the captain interjected but then stumbled around for words.

"It's not that simple, Detective," Tillian said. "I'm only here to ask a couple of questions about Steve Holcomb."

"Okay, ask," Mike said as he sat down in his chair.

"Can you tell me what Holcomb said when you questioned him about dreams?"

"Dreams? What exactly do you mean by dreams?" Detective Long asked. He wanted to find out a little more from Tillian.

"Yes, dreams. As when one goes to sleep and has a dream. I know he mentioned to you he was able to control his dreams. I'm curious as to what else he might have said," Colonel Tillian said.

Detective Long started believing something other than a kid stealing a car was going on. "Colonel, what's this about?" Mike asked again, feeling frustrated with the conversation.

"Detective, I'm trying to find out some information, and you would be well advised to cooperate with me." Tillian spoke as if he was getting tired of being questioned by the detective.

"So the government is getting into dreams nowadays?" Detective Long asked with a smirk.

"Detective, what else did the kid say about dreams?" Colonel Tillian asked more forcefully.

"Okay. Since you seem to already know, I'll tell you. The kid has mental issues. He told us a lady gave him the car he stole because he was able to control her reality by using her dreams against her. As far as the money goes, we still don't know where that came from. Who knows? He might have dreamed that also. That pretty much sums it up." Mike and his captain glanced at each other when they noticed Tillian was lost in his thoughts. "And why is the government here to investigate a kid with mental problems?" the detective asked.

"And did he say anything about having friends or anyone else having this ability?" Tillian asked without answering Mike's question.

"You believe his story?" Mike asked, shocked by Tillian's question.

Colonel Tillian adamantly kept questioning Long. "Please, Detective, was there anyone else involved regarding the dreams?"

Chuckling out loud and shaking his head with disbelief, Detective Long stood up from his chair and went over to his file cabinet to get the paperwork he had on Steve and tossed it on the desk.

The captain picked up the file but didn't look at it. "Is this your report?" he asked the detective.

"Yes, why?" Long asked.

"One more thing, Detective. The charges have been dropped, and you no longer need to worry about Holcomb," Colonel Tillian told Mike as he stood up and took the folder from the captain, who handed it to him without question.

"What the hell are you referring to?" Detective Long questioned, raising his voice.

"Mike, it's out of my hands now," his captain said as Tillian left the detective's office.

"What the hell do you mean, out of your hands?" Mike barked at his captain.

"Precisely that. So let it go." With that, his captain left the office as well.

Mike slammed the door after his captain left, but the door was opened again as his partner, Dale Yoder, came into the office. "What's all the commotion about?" Dale asked. "And who was the person who just left your office?"

"They took us off the Holcomb case," Long said and then summarized his conversation with Tillian.

"Why is the government involved?" Yoder asked.

"I'm not sure, but I sure know damn well where to find out!" Mike said angrily, and he left his office with Detective Yoder following.

Pulling up in front of Lifelong, Mike and Dale got out of the car, showed their badges to the guard, and went inside.

"What the hell did you tell them?" Detective Long demanded of Jerry Maiden.

"So you just barge into people's offices now, Mike?" Dr. Maiden asked. Dr. Maiden knew why they had come to see him. "The kid needs the kind of help I'm unable to give him," Jerry said sincerely.

Detective Long shook his head. "Anyone can tell the kid needs help. You're a psychiatrist. What do you mean you can't help him?"

"He doesn't have mental issues," Jerry spoke compassionately, using a tone he might use if he were speaking to one of his patients.

Detective Yoder's eyes opened wide in surprise. "Are you serious? You believe his story?"

Maiden indicated two chairs and told them to sit down. "Mike, I can get into trouble for what I'm going to share with you. But knowing you as I do, you won't let it rest until you find yourself in trouble for trying to uncover what's going on." Jerry let the detectives contemplate how serious the matter could be for them, and then he explained, "Years ago, I was a psychiatrist in the military. I was assigned to be on a team with

Colonel Tillian. We did studies on individuals for a few years together. My function was evaluating a person to find out if his or her mind would be able to handle the experiment and also to monitor the person's mental state afterward. Eventually, I saw how the minds of these individuals were becoming warped because of the medicines and the experiments. After raising a concern, I was taken off the project and eventually resigned from the service, at which time I was warned that project Dream Catcher didn't exist."

"Dream Catcher?" Detective Yoder asked.

Jerry nodded slowly and finally said, "The government wanted to know if dreams could be controlled."

"If you're going to get into trouble for telling us this, then why are you telling us now?" Mike asked.

"To warn you," the doctor said.

"To warn us?" Yoder spoke up.

"Yes. The reason the project I worked on was a failure is because none of the individuals could control their dreams. However, that was just the first part of the project."

"The first part?" Yoder asked.

Maiden nodded again, but didn't look at either detective as he explained, "The second part was to find out if our test subjects could get into someone else's dream."

Mike smiled slowly as he figured out the rest of the story. "And this capability to enter into someone's dream was just the beginning. Eventually, it was used against the person, wasn't it? And this kid has that ability, and Colonel Tillian wants it."

"I'm afraid so," Dr. Maiden said worriedly.

"Okay, so now we know what Tillian's motivation was for getting his hands on Holcomb, but what did you mean about warning us?" Detective Long inquired.

"Tillian told me the project was scrapped because it was unsuccessful. But after talking with him yesterday, I believe the project was a success."

"Which means, they're in the second part of the project," Detective Yoder said, finishing Maiden's sentence.

"What makes you believe the project is still going on?" Yoder asked Maiden.

"I do have a degree in psychology. You might say I'm somewhat trained in understanding people and their behaviors." Maiden smiled at Yoder. "Tillian was acting oddly when we talked about the project and Holcomb, so I believe he is still involved somehow, and they are in the second phase." Jerry was sure he'd read Tillian correctly. "And besides … what better way to take the project to the next stage? Say it was a failure—and then take it underground, so to speak," Jerry said, as if he was well aware of what was going on.

"That would explain his interest in Holcomb," Long said.

"Yes. And that's another reason why I believe the project is still very much alive," Jerry told them.

"I'll be a son of a bitch," Yoder said in astonishment. "The kid was telling the truth."

"Yes, Detective Yoder, Steve Holcomb was telling the truth," Dr. Maiden said.

"So where's the kid now?" Detective Long inquired.

"Tillian already took him," Maiden responded.

"*What?* Knowing this bullshit, why on earth did you hand the kid over to Tillian?" Detective Long asked in frustration.

"With the ability this kid has, I couldn't just let him run around the streets," Jerry Maiden said in his own defense.

"No, but if we could have kept him locked up in a jail for the felony, he couldn't do any more damage than what he has already done," Mike responded.

Jerry Maiden walked over to stare out the window as he thought about how to reply to Detective Long.

"Well?" the detective asked, waiting for the reply.

"Eventually, he would have gotten into the guards' dreams and gotten out. Then where would you be?" Jerry said with a

word of warning as he stared at Detective Long. "And Mike, although you don't believe it, this is the best place for the boy,"
Jerry spoke with conviction.

"And why is that?" Detective Yoder questioned.

"When we were doing our studies, we felt that if the subjects
could see our faces, then they could get into our dreams and
influence us in some way. So we kept hoods over them while
testing and ensured they didn't have any contact with anyone.
Tillian has the facilities to keep him isolated," Jerry said.

"How is that better?" Mike Long asked.

"Think about it for a moment. If you had the ability to control someone's dream, don't you think you eventually might be
able to influence his or her reality, just as Holcomb claimed
he did? And if the wrong person has the ability to do that ..."
Jerry stopped talking to let the detectives ponder what could
happen.

"Mike, if the kid's telling the truth, and the doc here is back-
ing up his story, we've just handed over three more test subjects
for Tillian's experiments," Detective Yoder said, reminding Mike
that Tillian had the names of the rest of us.

Detective Long looked at Yoder with a sigh.

"So there are more of them," Maiden said flatly.

"I'm sure I'll have more questions for you, Jerry," Detective
Long said, and then he and his partner left the institute.

That night, Detective Long tossed and turned in bed, unable
to sleep. He heard Suzie, his six-year-old niece who was down
the hall, crying. His wife asked him if Suzie was keeping him
awake.

"No," he answered, "I've been thinking of a case I'm working on."

His wife kissed him good night and said, "You'll work it out;
you always do."

Detective Long eventually went to check on Suzie, although she had stopped crying. Peeking in the door to her room, he saw her sleeping but still moving restlessly in bed.

"Mike, I'm sorry if she's keeping you awake," Jennifer, his sister, said quietly as she sat on a chair inside Suzie's room.

"She's fine, sis," he reassured his sister. He closed the door and left his sister to tend to his niece. He knew now what he was going to do regarding us and, hopefully, Steve.

That next morning when I walked out of the house to pick up Bobby for school, Detective Long was waiting outside, leaning against my car.

"Morning, David," he said politely, startling me.

"Detective?" I responded with caution, wondering why he was here so early.

"I would like to talk with you a little bit, if you don't mind." He sounded unsure if I would agree.

I didn't want to talk to him, so I said, "I'm going to be late for school and need to go."

Before I could get into my car, he asked, "Whose dream did you go into last night?"

I looked back at him, feeling as if I had been caught doing something I should not have been doing. I hesitated to even respond to his question.

"I don't understand it, but I'm pretty sure you and your friends do have a gift when it comes to dreams," he said as I tried not to make eye contact.

"Detective ..." I began.

"Don't worry," he assured me with a smile, "I'm not here to take you to Lifelong."

"Is that where Steve is?" I snapped at him.

"I can't answer that," he said, but the way he took his eyes off me confirmed my suspicions. "I want to know if it's true. Can you control dreams?"

"Just a moment ago you said you were sure I did. Now you don't know?" I tried to avoid telling him the truth.

"I guess the best thing to do, in order for us to talk, is to tell you there's a Colonel Tillian who might be looking for you and your friends."

Mike's words were intended to keep me interested in the conversation. It worked. Concerned, I scanned the surrounding area.

He smirked. "If they're here, you're not going to know where they are," the detective said, seeing how worried I seemed.

"Won't you get into trouble for telling me this?" I asked.

He shrugged his shoulders as if to say he didn't care, and then he started walking toward his car, leaving me standing there.

"Why would a colonel want us?" I called after him.

Detective Long stopped and turned toward me. "Kid, you may not have time to play this. I just want to know for myself if you can or can't. As for me, personally, I'm starting to believe you can." He opened his car door without looking my way.

"Why is it important to you if I can or can't?" I countered.

Looking back at me, he smiled and said, "You and your friend Steve are alike." He walked back toward me, saying sternly, "If you do have the gift, you shouldn't be going around messing with a person's life."

"We quit doing that," I retorted. It made me angry that he accused me of something he knew nothing about. But I couldn't believe it. I had opened my mouth once again without thinking of the consequences and had given him the answer he wanted. "Now what? You're going to haul me to Lifelong too?" I asked as I walked closer to my car door.

"No. I have no desire to send you or your friends there," he replied.

"It didn't take you long to send Steve there, did it?" I said angrily.

"I did what I felt was best for Steve."

I'd asked him what was next for my friends and me—and that's when he pulled out his wallet and handed me a photo of a little girl, telling me he wanted us to do something for him.

Once he explained what he wanted, he left, leaving me to wonder if we were about to walk into a trap. I picked up Bobby and called Rae. We met at the school parking lot, where I conveyed to them what Detective Long had requested.

"Why does he want us to go into his dream?" Bobby asked.

"I'm not sure," I replied. "It doesn't make sense to me either. I'm just as confused as you are."

"So who's the little girl in the photo?" Rae asked.

"Again, I'm not sure. I just know he wants us to go into his dream and take him into hers."

"Why doesn't he just take us to Lifelong as he did to Steve?" Rae wondered.

"We could always deny what we can do," I informed them. "I'm sure they couldn't hold us. They're holding Steve because he told them what he could do—that's the difference." And then I remembered something else. "One more thing he said—there's a Colonel Tillian who may be looking for us."

"David, we're in a great deal of trouble, aren't we?" Rae's voice was shaky.

"We're into something bad. And I think Long has a clue, and he doesn't want to tell us—at least for now," I replied, feeling just as worried as Bobby and Rae were.

"What are we going to do?" Bobby asked. "How are we going to get out of this mess?"

I stood there looking at both of them, unable to answer Bobby's question.

Rae considered our options, saying, "My thought is to go along with what he wants. Who knows? Maybe it will be to our benefit somehow."

We all went to our classes, although we were unable to concentrate on schoolwork.

It's interesting that all through the school year I walked past other students I didn't know and never thought twice about them. But now, as I looked at each one, my mind started playing tricks on me, leading me to believe they were working for this Tillian person, spying on us as we went through the day. Although we were concerned with what Detective Long told me about Tillian, we made it through the school day without any incidents. Still, thinking we could easily be followed kept me in a paranoid state. But Tillian didn't seem to be too concerned about us for the time being.

Wearing ankle cuffs and handcuffs, a prison uniform, and a hood over his face, Steve walked as best as he could, still feeling unsteady from the sedatives he was given. Military guards, who wore black masks, escorted him to an interrogation room. They led him to the chair in the middle of the room, facing a mirror on the wall. The guards strapped Steve's feet and hands to the chair, removed the hood, and then left the room.

"You bastards. Let me go!" Steve shouted as he tried struggling to get free of the chair. "What do you want from me?" He sat for long periods—it seemed like all day—but would shout over and over again, "Let my ass go!"

"I can't do that," a voice finally said through the speakers in the corner of the room.

"What do you want?" Steve said loudly.

"I want your gift of dream control," Tillian said from the other side of the mirror.

"I don't know what you're talking about" Steve replied unconvincingly and then struggled to get free of the chair again.

The door behind him opened up, and Steve tried to look behind him to see who it was, but he could only get a glimpse of legs walking toward him. "Bastard! Leave me alone!" Steve shouted as he fought against the person who put the hood over his head. Although he was breathing hard and trying to catch his breath under the hood, he could hear more footsteps behind him.

After few minutes he heard the scraping of a chair across the floor and the sound of Colonel Tillian's voice as he sat in the chair facing Steve. "I'm sure you had a hard life growing up in foster homes," the colonel said in a compassionate tone.

"How do you know how I grew up?" Steve responded angrily.

Tillian placed a collection of photos on Steve's lap and lifted the hood high enough so that Steve could only see the pictures. "You know these people." Tillian spoke with certainty as Steve looked at the couples that had been his foster parents at one time or another.

"So? Who cares?" Steve said, uncaring.

"I care. I find it interesting that these three couples are currently in mental hospitals for evaluation, and I also find it very odd that these same people had a foster child telling detectives he has the ability to control dreams. So you tell me. Is it just a coincidence?" Tillian removed the pictures from Steve's lap.

Steve thought about what he'd done to his previous foster parents and started to sob underneath the hood. "I didn't mean to go that far; it just happened."

"You have no one left on your side to help you out of this mess," Colonel Tillian said considerately. "However, I can."

"We were just having fun in dreams."

"We?" the colonel asked.

"Yes, my friends. David, Rae, and Bobby," Steve said.

"Your friends denied they knew you had this gift," Tillian said. "You're here alone."

Steve felt abandoned as he thought about his family and friends. Steve finally stopped sobbing and said, "What do you want from me?"

"I want to do tests on you. That's all," Colonel Tillian said.

"What kind of tests?" Steve questioned.

"I want to study how you're able to control dreams."

"So you do believe me?" Steve asked.

"Why else would you be here if I didn't?" Colonel Tillian said.

"To lock my ass away in a nut farm," Steve said.

"If I didn't believe you, I would have left you back at Lifelong," Tillian said almost compassionately.

Steve started to become angry again when he realized he'd been taken somewhere else. "Where am I?" Steve asked, raising his voice.

"It doesn't matter at the moment."

"Damn you. Where the hell am I?" Steve shouted as he tried to get himself out of the chair.

Tillian waved the guards over to take Steve and then left the room.

"Let's go," one of the guards said, manhandling Steve to get him to calm down. He removed the wires from Steve's forehead and then replaced the hood over Steve's face before leading him out the door to his cell.

The door to his room was solid steel that had a six-by-six-inch two-way mirror—someone could look in, but Steve couldn't look out. Midway down the door was another opening large enough for Steve to place his hands through to be handcuffed before leaving the room. At the bottom of the door, about knee-high, there was a small door that could only be opened from the outside to squeeze small amounts of food through.

The door had no handles; it could only be opened electronically from another location in the building. "Open it up," one of the guards said into his hand radio to the guard who controlled the door. After a few seconds, the door started opening, sliding into the walls.

When the door shut and the handcuffs were removed, Steve was ordered to remove his hood and hand it to the guard through the small door. As Steve looked around, he saw the small ledge on the door where his food would be delivered. He walked over to it and tried pushing the door open to see out but was unable to.

In one corner of the room was a small cot, about a foot above the floor that was to be used as his bed. Next to the bed was a plastic stand that had pictures of a sophisticated man and woman. There weren't any windows in the room, but there was another door, although there was no handle or doorknob on it. "I could go to the bathroom!" Steve shouted up to one of the cameras that hung from the corner of the ceiling, believing the door led to the bathroom. A few second later, the bathroom door opened up by sliding into the wall.

After walking through the door, it rolled back out of the wall. Seeing there weren't any cameras in the restroom, Steve relieved himself. Looking around the door, Steve found a button to push, and the door opened. He went to the cot and picked up the photos.

After a few hours, Steve started dozing off. A man's voice came through the speaker telling him to stay awake. "Come on!" Steve shouted and rolled back over on the cot and closed his eyes.

"I said, stay awake!" the voice spoke again through the speakers.

"The hell with you," Steve said as he lay there with his eyes still closed. The door to his cell opened, and two hooded guards came in with batons, threatening him.

Tillian had set it up for Steve to be in a room where he wouldn't have contact with anyone at all, other than the eyes and ears of the cameras that watched every move he made. And guards would be sent in from time to time to ensure that Steve wasn't sleeping—not just yet.

Tillian walked to the lounge just outside the cafeteria in the building where he spotted Lieutenant Julie Miller, who was wearing her robe and drinking coffee. "Good morning, Lieutenant," Tillian greeted her.

"Good morning, sir," Julie replied, starting to stand up.

He waved his hand to keep her seated. "How are you feeling?" Tillian asked.

"Slow, but starting to get my bearings," she answered and took another sip of her coffee.

"How long was I asleep?"

"A few days," Tillian replied.

"It seems like eternity in there."

"I bet it does, with no sense of time." Tillian smiled at her. "I have an assignment for you." He showed her a picture of Steve.

"Who is he?" Julie asked.

"I'll explain later. Right now, get some solid food in you, and we'll talk later," the colonel told her and left.

Later that night, Steve's door opened, and a voice from the speakers instructed him to follow the blue line, one of four colored lines painted on the floor. Cameras and speakers were placed throughout the halls, watching Steve, or anyone else for that matter. Steve saw other doors along the hall, but when he started approaching one of the doors, a woman's voice rang out through the speakers, telling him to get away. Steve followed the blue line through the hall until he was told to stop. He'd reached the room where he was going to be sleeping for the night.

Men and women greeted Steve in doctor scrubs and surgical masks. Steve was escorted to a bed in the middle of the room and instructed to lie down. Steve looked around for another door that would allow him to escape. To the left, monitors hung on walls, lining up with the computers on desks below.

The wall in front of him had a mirror that was about three feet in width and height. As soon as Steve saw it, he knew someone would be watching from the other side, monitoring everything in the room. Surrounding the two-way mirror, more electronic equipment filled just about every space. To the wall on the right were computers, monitors, and additional equipment.

Looking back at the door where he'd come in, Steve saw a hooded person in a military uniform. "She said lie down," the male guard said, lifting his weapon so Steve could see it. He lay down on the bed, and his legs and arms were strapped down, preventing him from moving. Bending his head a little bit, Steve stared into the mirror as wires were connected all over his body.

Someone stood next to him with a syringe in her hand, and someone else connected a leather strap with wires around his head. A woman's voice spoke just above Steve's head. "He's ready."

"Sir, they're ready," Lieutenant Karen Mitchell said to Tillian from the room just behind the mirror. Steve's room was one of many rooms that encompassed the small observation room in the middle of the infirmary.

"Tell them to start," Tillian replied to the lieutenant and then walked out a door and went to Lieutenant Miller—she was in a room similar to the one Steve had.

"Sir," Lieutenant Julie Miller said, acknowledging Tillian.

"Lieutenant," he responded. "Are you feeling okay?"

"Sir, I'm a little confused about what you want me to do exactly," Julie said.

"I just want you to follow without him knowing. I need to know if he really does have the abilities he claims. If he tries to make contact with anyone, find out who and then break the connection," Tillian told her.

"Yes, sir," she said and then she was injected with the drug, as Steve had been.

CHAPTER 7 DREAMERS

Bobby, Rae, and I decided to meet at the pond in our dreams to start what Detective Long had requested. "Remember, he may not be asleep yet," I told them, and then I thought of the detective's face to open the door to his dream. Rae decided to focus on the dream of the little girl who was in the photo she'd seen in reality.

Thinking about the girl, Rae waved her hand in front of her and a portal started opening up, revealing a park in the distance. Not seeing anyone, she walked out of the shadow of the dream and went over to the swings that were next to the merry-go-round. "Well, hello there," Rae said to the little girl she saw on the merry-go-round. From the photo, Rae knew it was the same girl who Detective Long wanted us to see in dreams.

The girl pushed herself around again. "Are you from the wind?" the girl asked when she came back around to where Rae was standing.

"Wind? No, I'm not from the wind," Rae replied, wondering what the girl meant.

"Oh, I thought you might be one of the faces I see." The girl went around in a circle again.

"Are you here by yourself?" Rae asked.

"Yes. I always come here alone. This is my hiding place." She smiled as she continued go around on the merry-go-round.

"Hiding place?" Rae questioned as she sat on the ground, waiting for the girl to slowly come back around. "What are you hiding from?"

The girl gave Rae a smile as she went past her again, sitting on the edge of the merry-go-round.

"Where are your mommy and daddy?" Rae asked. "Why are you here by yourself?"

Coming back around to Rae, the little girl stopped in front of her. "Mommy never comes here with me. I tell her I'm scared, but she doesn't come to help me," the girl whispered in a scared voice.

"What's your name?" Rae questioned.

"Suzie." The girl went around again.

"Hi, Suzie. I'm Rae," she said, smiling.

"Suzie, why are you scared?" Before the little girl could answer, Rae felt the wind pick up around them. Darkness started to encompass the playground, moving in toward Rae and Suzie.

"We need to stay on the merry-go-round. They won't know we are here if we stay here and don't move," Suzie told Rae as she moved to the center of the merry-go-round.

"They? Who are they?" Rae questioned as she saw the darkness getting closer.

"The faces and voices," Suzie said as she sat there, tightly clutching her knees with her arms. "You have to get on here now!" she shouted at Rae and started crying.

Rae heeded the girl's cry and stepped on the merry-go-round, sitting down in the middle next to Suzie.

The merry-go-round moved with the wind, and Rae held onto Suzie as they started spinning faster and faster. Rae saw the darkness had stopped coming closer to them and rested a few feet away from the merry-go-round. After a few moments, as they were still swirling around, faces slowly started to appear inside the cloud of darkness. Rae looked down at Suzie, who had her face hidden between her knees, her ears covered, and her eyes tightly closed.

"Get your ass to bed," the voices said in unison as faces started coming into focus. "Damn it, I said bed," the voices spoke again. "You think you need anything to eat? You don't deserve supper." Rae heard the voices shouting louder. With the merry-go-round still moving fast, Rae stood up as best as she could, holding on to the bars. She could see the many faces of the same man all around in the whirlwind. The voices and faces spoke again as they merged into one face in front of Rae, looking down towards Suzie. "You're just like your mother—lazy and not worth shit."

"I'm sorry, Daddy. I'll try to do better," Suzie cried out, still covering her face. "Please, Daddy, don't hit me again. I didn't mean to drop the glass. It slipped."

While Rae was inside the girl's dream, Bobby and I had finally made contact with Detective Long's dream and brought him into our dream. Suddenly, I heard Steve's voice in the distance. "David!" Steve called. "David!"

"Here, Steve," I replied, and the vortex opened up, connecting our dreams together. "Where are you?" I questioned him, surprised to see him.

Steve spoke in fear. "A Colonel Tillian has me somewhere. I'm not sure where, but I need your help. Please."

"How can we help if I don't know where you are?" I asked, as his farmhouse started becoming clearer in the background.

"You got me into this mess! Now get my ass out of here!" Steve shouted angrily.

When he wouldn't listen to me and come through the gateway, I decided to step through to his dream. And that's when I noticed something I hadn't seen in dreams before.

"Is someone there with you?" I asked as I saw a shadow lingering in the distance of his dream. He turned around to get a better look.

"Who the hell are you?" Steve shouted toward the shadow.

"Steve!" I shouted as the gateway between our dreams closed.

After Steve's dream vanished, I stood there looking at Bobby and Detective Long, who seemed to be oblivious to everything. Then we heard Rae scream our names. "David! Bobby!" Rae shouted again. After Bobby created a gateway to Rae in Suzie's dream, we stepped through and then heard Rae screaming somewhere beyond the whirlwind.

"Oh, my God! Stop! *Stop!*" Rae screamed as hand marks appeared on Suzie's arms, as if someone was squeezing them and trying to pull Suzie's hands away from her face.

"Rae!" I shouted, trying to find her in the darkness of the wind.

And then, just as loudly as we heard Rae's screams, we saw what Rae was seeing. "Just for that ..." the man's voice boomed. Suzie's head moved side to side, as if someone was slapping her face.

"Daddy, please stop!" Suzie cried as tears flowed down her cheeks, where hand welts suddenly appeared.

"Stop! You're hurting her!" Rae's voice shrieked in fear, seeing hand welts all over the little girl's face.

Bobby and I both started thrusting our hands toward the whirlwind, casting out balls of energy. The energy exploded inside the whirlwind, ripping it to pieces until it was gone. As we came closer to the merry-go-round, we saw Rae bending down, grabbing at Suzie just as she faded, leaving Rae on the merry-go-round, spinning alone.

"Rae?" I said quietly. I headed for the merry-go-round, just as Rae looked at me and then vanished.

Rae woke up in her bed crying.

"What the hell was that?" Bobby asked, fearing it might come back.

Looking at Detective Long, I could tell he was just like any other dreamer who went along passively in dreams. No matter what was happening, dreamers were unaware of the dream they were in. "I'm dreaming." The detective sobbed, and then he faded. Bobby and I stood there, feeling lost and confused ... and then we woke up from the nightmare we just were in.

Detective Long sat up quickly in bed, looking around. He went to Suzie's room to check on her, only to find she was already out of bed. When he got to the kitchen, Mrs. Long saw the worried expression on his face. "Honey, what's the matter?" she asked.

Instead of answering his wife, he walked over to Suzie. "Sweetie, are you hurt?"

"No, Uncle Mikey," Suzie said.

His sister, Jennifer, looked at him quizzically. "Mike, why would Suzie be hurt?"

"I had a bad dream about Suzie," Mike explained. "I don't remember what exactly happened. I just woke up thinking she was hurt."

"Well, she did have another nightmare last night," Jennifer told her brother.

Mike knew that Suzie had been having nightmares, and they seemed to have gotten worse since his sister left her husband, months ago.

"I've taken her to get counseling," Jennifer said, "but she tells them she doesn't remember her dreams, other than she thinks they are always the same. I just don't know what to do."

"Rae?" I said tenderly when I called her after I woke up. I could hear her sniffles on the other end of the line. Rae lay on her bed, resting her phone upon her cheek, not saying a word. "Rae?" I said again.

"I didn't see anyone touching her," she answered, still crying. I let her talk as I lay there listening to her breath quietly, eventually falling back to sleep.

Steve opened his eyes cussing and screaming at anyone who might be there. "You bastards! Who was following me?"

In the next room over, Lieutenant Miller also woke up from her sleep. "Get me some water," she commanded one of the nurses. After taking a drink of water, she walked out of her room and into Steve's room, where he was shouting as a doctor injected something into him, putting him back to sleep.

Steve woke in the morning to the sounds of people in his infirmary room. He saw they were reading charts and monitors.

"Good; you're awake," a nurse said as she started loosening the straps that were used to tie Steve down. "Just follow the blue line back to your room," she instructed him.

Steve still felt a little incoherent from the drugs they'd given him, but he did what he was told without question. Reaching his room, he sat on the cot. The door closed behind him.

Tillian found Lieutenant Miller waiting for him outside his office, as ordered. "Good morning, sir," she said, rising up from a chair.

"Morning, Lieutenant. Come in," he told her as he went into his office. "Were you able to see who Birch is?"

"Yes, sir," she replied. Then she asked, "Sir, if I may? How did you know Holcomb would contact the other kid?"

"I didn't. But I had my suspicions he would, and that's why I wanted you to follow him. This tells me that both he and Birch have the capabilities of communicating with each other in dreams. And that's what I needed to find out." Tillian leaned back in his chair as she stood there, looking confused.

"Also, I needed you to see Birch so that if what I thought was true, you'd be able to track him. Are you able to?" the colonel asked excitedly.

"Yes, sir, but I'm confused as to why I still need to follow Holcomb. Don't you already have photos of him for me to look at?" she asked.

"No, we don't, but the best proof is that you verified Holcomb and Birch have the same abilities, and they were able to communicate with each other in dreams," he said arrogantly. "That's all, Lieutenant." The colonel looked down at the reports on his desk.

"Sir, will I be following Holcomb tonight?"

"No, I want you to get back to your duties but also keep track of Birch," the colonel told her.

"Yes, sir," she replied and headed toward the door.

"Oh, Lieutenant," he said as he looked up from his desk.

"Sir?" she responded.

"This is confidential. Is that clear, Lieutenant?"

"Yes, sir," Lieutenant Miller responded and then left.

The data from Steve's dream was analyzed by the doctors and reported back to Tillian. After a few hours of discussion with doctors, Tillian ordered Steve's cell door opened. "Follow the yellow line," a man's voice came through the speakers in his room. Steve followed the yellow line down the hall and saw two guards, wearing hoods and carrying weapons, standing at the door to the interrogation room. They walked Steve inside, sat him down in the chair, and began to strap him in as they had the day before.

"Good morning." Tillian's voice came from the speakers. "Did you have a restful night?"

Steve spoke harshly. "Who was that spying on me in my dream?"

"In time. Now, my first question ... how did you make contact with David?" the colonel asked. Steve didn't answer. "Please answer the question." Steve refused to answer and sat there looking around the room. "If you don't answer, I'll guarantee that you will not wake up from your next dream," Tillian threatened. "I'll make sure the next time you go to sleep, it will be a nightmare." Without hesitation, Tillian said, "Guards!" Two hooded guards outside the door came in and stood close to Steve. "Mr. Holcomb, it's really up to you how easy this is going to be," Tillian said sternly. "Now, how did you make contact with David?"

Steve sighed heavily. "All I did was call his name."

"That's all? Just call his name?" Tillian asked.

"Yes," Steve admitted reluctantly.

"Does Birch have the same capabilities you have?" Tillian asked.

When Steve hesitated, one of the guards moved closer to him with his baton out. "Yes, damn it!" Steve shouted toward the guard.

"How about Mr. Eriks and Miss Woods? Do they also have the ability to control dreams?"

"Yes, okay?" Steve said, wanting the questions to stop.

"So when you called Birch, it took both of you to make a dream connection?" Tillian questioned.

"Not always," Steve replied.

"Not always? What do you mean?" Tillian wanted to know.

"I don't have to call David's name to get into his dreams. I can think of his face, and then I'm there. We call each other's names out of courtesy—something I'm not getting here," Steve said derisively.

"That's all for today," Tillian said.

"Who the hell was in my dream?" Steve shouted, demanding an answer.

Guards walked in and took Steve back to his cell. After returning to his cell, Steve saw the same photos, along with a note telling him to concentrate on the pictures and that if he didn't comply with the instructions in the note, he wouldn't wake up from his dream. Steve knew what Tillian wanted, but Steve wasn't sure if that was how he wanted to spend his dreams anymore. Then again, if he didn't do as Tillian demanded, he knew he wasn't going to get out of there. He decided to comply with Tillian's orders, but there was one thing he was able to do that no one would know.

Rae, Bobby, and I met Detective Long to talk about Suzie's dream. "Who was the little girl?" Rae asked sadly.

"She's my niece." He told us that Suzie had been having nightmares over the last few years, but lately, they'd been getting worse.

We brought the detective up to speed on what happened in Suzie's dream.

"I do remember part of it," he told us after we finished our story. "I remember you were talking to someone before we went into Suzie's dream."

"Steve," I said.

He looked at me strangely. "You can still communicate with him?"

"Only for a short time," I said.

Detective Long nodded. "I remember feeling helpless because I couldn't do anything to help Suzie."

"That's one of the perks of doing what we do. We don't feel helpless," Bobby said with a smile.

"Not always," Rae spoke. She still felt as if she'd let Suzie down. "Do you have a picture of Suzie and her family?" Rae asked the detective.

"Sure." He pulled out a wallet-size photo of Suzie with her dad, Jim, and her mother.

After studying the picture, Rae handed it back to the detective. Bobby and I both had a feeling what she was planning, but neither one of us was about to tell Long or even tell Rae she shouldn't do something in her dreams.

"So you think she was being abused?" Bobby asked with concern.

"I'm not sure. But I will be paying my brother-in-law a visit," Detective Long told us.

I had one more question I needed answered. To me, dealing with Detective Long seemed too easy, but right now, he was our only link to finding Steve. "Detective, inside the dream, you said that you were dreaming and then you left. Can you control dreams?"

After taking time to consider his words, he shared with us that at times, in his dreams, he knew he was dreaming—but only to the extent of knowing. "But I don't have what you kids can do. And when Dr. Maiden confirmed Steve's ability, I was hoping you could help me see inside Suzie's dream to find out what's going on."

"Dr. Maiden?" Bobby asked with interest.

"I appreciate you kids doing this for me, but I can't talk about Mr. Holcomb's situation," Detective Long responded.

"Steve contacted me just before we went into Suzie's dream," I said. "He said Tillian has him somewhere and he needs help. Why can't you tell us what's going on? We helped you; why can't you help us?" I didn't appreciate his unwillingness to help Steve or us.

"It's not that I don't want to help. I just don't know what to do, especially with Tillian's involvement," he replied defensively.

"I can help Suzie," Rae spoke, breaking the tense mood between the detective and me.

"How do you mean?" Detective Long questioned Rae.

"Her dream. I think I know a way to stop them," Rae said.

"How do you propose to do that?" Long asked, seeming hopeful.

Although Rae could keep going into Suzie's dream every night to help Suzie fight the dream, it would eventually take its toll on Rae. Rae smiled without answering the detective's question.

Bobby questioned our abilities to move freely in the streets. "Why hasn't Tillian come for us?"

"My guess is that he's trying to find out all he can through Steve, and then ..." Detective Long stopped speaking to let us think about what he was saying about our future.

Later that night, we were sitting in Rae's backyard, talking. "There's one thing I didn't tell you guys," I said, the concern clear in my voice. "When I was talking with Steve, I saw some-one else—a shadow."

"Who?" Bobby immediately questioned.

"Maybe it was just a dreamer in his dream," Rae said casually.

"No, I don't think so. When I asked Steve about the shadow, he looked around and starting shouting 'Who the hell are you?' and our dream connection was lost. Whoever it was acted as if he was following Steve."

"You know what?" Bobby said seriously, giving me a hard look. "This is getting too weird for me. I think I need a few nights of my own dreams—of mansions and women and not worrying about this shit any longer. What used to be fun is now becoming too involved with Tillian and the cops." He said good-bye and headed home.

"Maybe Bobby is right. Things are getting strange," I told Rae.

"It is, but right now, I need to help Suzie," she said sorrowfully.

Bobby's words kept coming to mind as I lay in bed; I felt the same way he did. Our dreams were supposed to be fun, but now, they'd taken on a whole new meaning, and none of us knew how to deal with it.

But Steve was our friend, and it was my fault he was in this predicament. I couldn't just leave him alone. I wanted to find out what was going on and how Tillian was involved. As I started to fall asleep, I wondered what Tillian was hiding, and who the person was hiding in the shadow of Steve's dream.

Rae had talked with Mary, and then she went to her bed, thinking of Suzie. Rae was prepared as to what to expect in Suzie's nightmare, but she just wasn't sure how far in her dream Suzie already was. As Rae stood by the pond in her dream, she took a deep breath, and a gateway opened, revealing the whirl-wind already heading toward Suzie as she sat on the merry-go-round, screaming for it to go away.

Instantly, Rae stood next to the merry-go-round, watching the darkness come closer. Rae stopped the merry-go-round and climbed toward the center to Suzie. "Suzie, it's me," Rae said, trying to get Suzie to take her face away from her knees and look up at her.

"Rae? Rae?" Rae barely heard Mary's voice as the winds picked up faster and louder.

"Mary!" Rae responded, and then another door opened up, just next to the merry-go-round.

"Wow!" Mary exclaimed, surprised by what she was seeing.

"Suzie, please look up," Rae begged her. "You don't have to be scared anymore."

"I'm hiding!" Suzie cried.

"Rae, it's getting closer!" Mary shouted to Rae over the winds. "Now?" Mary started raising her hands up.

"No! She has to see it first!" Rae shouted back at Mary.

She begged Suzie again, "Suzie, please look up."

"I can't." Suzie started crying.

"Get your ass to bed," the voices said in unison as the faces started to come into focus. "Damn it, I said bed!"

As Rae sat with Suzie on the merry-go-round, the faces of Suzie's father started coming into focus all around them.

"Rae!" Mary shouted again over the noise, trying to get her sister to hurry up.

"Suzie, if you look up, they will go away," Rae said, still speaking compassionately to Suzie.

Suzie looked up, but she screamed as she saw the faces.

"Now!" Rae shouted at Mary as she held Suzie's face up to keep her watching.

Mary started to raise her hands again when she heard Rae say, "Don't wake up, sweetie." Rae tried to keep Suzie focused on the wind. "Mary, hurry." Rae's voice grew in a fury.

As Mary saw Suzie's body start to fade from Rae's arms, she jumped on the merry-go-round and touched Suzie's forehead, and then focused on the whirlwind.

"You think you need anything to eat? You don't deserve supper!" the voices said.

"Now!" Rae shouted again. Suzie opened her eyes, looking at the whirlwind and screaming.

"You're just like your mom—lazy and not worth shit!" the voices said as the faces merged into one.

The merry-go-round stopped moving, and Mary spoke casually at the face in front of her. "Shut the hell up."

"Damn it, Mary, just do it!" Rae screamed at her sister. While the wind blew all around and darkness still encompassed them, the three of them stood in stillness on the merry-go-round.

Raising her hands, Mary caused the sky above them to become bright orange, and then a breeze started in the center of the merry-go-round, blowing Suzie's hair in her eyes. Rae moved the hair back, away from Suzie's eyes, as Mary's whirlwind grew in strength. "Suzie, keep looking, sweetie," Rae said excitedly, trying to get her to watch what Mary was doing. As the winds picked up from the center, they started spinning faster and faster as they reached the edge of the merry-go-round, where Mary stood looking into the face of Suzie's nightmare.

The sky now turned bright red, and Rae and Suzie saw lightning flash above them and then heard the thunder getting louder with each strike of lightning. Mary chanted more words. As the wind from Mary pushed outward, moving in the opposite direction, it finally reached the other whirlwind with full force. Seeing more lightning and hearing more cracks of the thunder, Rae and Suzie both watched as the bolts struck the whirlwind.

Mary brought her hands down and clapped them together, pointing them toward the whirlwind as the lightning bolts increased along with the thunder, crashing all around them outside the merry-go-round area. And then, with determination on her face, Mary made one final push of her winds, as the palms of her hands pointed toward the face in the wind. Instantly, all the lightning bolts, fire from her palms, and her storm exploded on the face, smashing and scattering its pieces into the air where lightning soon struck them before they could hit the ground. "God, I love dream world," Mary said, grinning as she looked back toward Rae and Suzie, who were just staring at her in wonder.

"Where did it go?" Suzie questioned in awe.

Rae pulled Suzie closer to her and hugged her. "It's gone for good, sweetie," Rae responded as she continued hugging and rocking Suzie. Rae believed that if Suzie could watch her nightmare go away while she was still dreaming, Suzie wouldn't have the dream any more. "I have something I need to do," Rae told Suzie and then looked over to Mary, who was still grinning at what she did.

Mary walked over to the center of the merry-go-round and said, "Hi, Suzie. Do you like unicorns?" Mary held Suzie's hand and faded from Rae's sight. Rae knew that Suzie would spend the rest of her dream riding unicorns in Mary's wonderland dream.

For a few nights, Mary would visit Suzie's dreams, just to ensure she wasn't having the nightmare, and then she would take her riding again. And each morning, Suzie would wake up happy.

After Mary and Suzie left Rae in the remnants of Suzie's dream, she opened another portal and walked through. "That bastard!" Rae said as she stood in the shadows of a bedroom where Jim, Suzie's father, was lying in bed with someone other than Jennifer.

"Well, hello," Jim said, smiling at Rae as she came out of the shadows of Jim's dream.

"Can you handle both of us?" Rae replied with a smile.

"Oh, I'm sure I can," came his conceited reply.

"Well, let's see what you got," Rae said. The blankets on the bed moved by themselves, exposing Jim, but the woman with him held up sheets around her neck, screaming in horror at what she just saw. Jim looked down and started screaming also—the lower half of his body was slowly dissolving in front of him.

"I guess we're alone," Rae said, smiling, when the woman next to Jim disappeared from Jim's dream as he started to wake up. "Oh, no. You don't want to leave now," Rae said. "We're just starting to have fun." She kept Jim from waking up from his nightmare and laughed at him as she used her dream magic to cuff his hands to the bedpost.

As Jim struggled to get free, Rae waved her hand, and Jim's lower body started to appear again—but it resembled snake-like heads that started biting his upper body. Rae walked over to the door and opened it, allowing light gray smoke to fill the room. With fear in his eyes, Jim stared at the hideous, creature-like women who floated through the smoke surrounding the bed. Some of the women had cut marks all over their bodies as blood seeped through their skin, and others had bloody welts protruding from their faces, as if they were stretching out toward Jim.

Jim screamed and closed his eyes so that he couldn't see the women, but Rae kissed his eyelids, making them transparent, which forced Jim to watch as other women floated into view. They all had hand marks and bruises on their faces and naked bodies, and they were laughing at him. Jim kept shouting for it to stop, but he heard their voices speak. "You good-for-nothing piece of shit. You have nothing for us anymore. You can't satisfy us." The ladies' voices spoke and laughed in harmony at him as they continued to circle his bed, watching the snakeheads continue to bite as he screamed.

As he lay there pleading for mercy, welts started appearing all over him while he was forced to watch his own body being beaten until the last possible moment of sleep.

Rae woke up in a sweat, thinking of what she just had done. She had done what she always had refused to do: she gave a dreamer a nightmare for her own purpose. She felt a little remorseful because she didn't know if Suzie's dad was actually abusing her, but after seeing what Suzie went through, Rae's anger took over, even though Jim might not have had anything to do with Suzie's dream.

Rae wasn't the only one giving nightmares that night. For the experiment, what Tillian had in store for Steve was just as bad in dreams but worse in reality.

"Mr. Holcomb." Tillian's voice came through the speaker. "I hope you understand the assignment and how important it is for you to follow the instructions to the letter."

"Yes," Steve said, and then he heard a woman's voice coming through the speakers, telling the doctor to proceed. Steve tried to move, but in the end, he soon felt himself falling asleep.

When Steve woke up from reality, he stood in front of his grayish farmhouse. As he looked around, the scenery started coming into focus as he stood there, wishing everything to come to life. Crop workers would suddenly appear, tilling the ground, just as cattle workers came into view, tending the cattle as he thought them into existence.

Content with what he saw, he walked up to the porch and sat down on the swing to admire his creation. It seemed the only time he enjoyed anything was when he was at his house. "I'm thirsty!" Steve shouted toward the wooden screen door. Looking out into the yard, the vision of a creek came into focus, winding through the grassy yard.

"Here you go, honey," Steve's mom said and she came out the door with lemonade. Steve didn't know the look of his real parents, but he kept the same image of the couple he'd first met at the farm as his parents.

"Thanks, Mom," he said, smiling at her, and then she vanished from view.

He believed he was being followed in his dream again but was unable to pinpoint the person. He figured he'd better start looking for the dream of the woman he'd seen in the photo. As he sat there drinking his lemonade, a door slowly opened up into her dream. It grew larger in front of him, but he sat there until the brightness that surrounded the gateway subsided. He had a view of the woman enjoying a barbeque with others. Steve set his drink down and floated, still in the sitting position, into her dream.

Once inside the dream, rain, wind, and hail started coming down around the cookout. People ran toward the house, and he saw the woman just as she too was about to go inside the make-believe home. He reached out his hand in her direction, stopping her from moving, just as he changed her dream vision to where they both stood in darkness.

"Your husband is cheating on you," he told the woman from somewhere in the darkness.

"Who are you?" she asked fearfully.

Steve released her from his grip; he knew she wasn't able to wake up just yet. "I'm here because you need to know the truth about your husband," Steve said, showing concern for the woman.

"What do you mean? And where are we?" she demanded to know. "I can't see anything!"

"Don't raise your voice at me," he responded, knocking her down with an unseen force.

"Why are you doing this?" she questioned in fear.

"*Why?*" he mocked her. "I'll tell you why. I'm sick and tired of being used and forgotten." He spoke with loathing in his voice. "I've had enough of being walked on, and if I have to show you this to get free of the torture that's inside of me, I will, even if I have to torment every dreamer."

A small red light started spinning around somewhere in the darkness, getting larger and producing a buzzing noise as it came closer to her. Eventually, the red circle was large enough to create a gateway encompassed by the circle as the light continued to spin.

Covering her ears from the buzzing sound of the gateway, the woman soon saw a face on the other side. "John?" she questioned if that was her husband. "Don't hurt him," she begged Steve.

"I won't," Steve said with a grin. "I just wanted to show you what he's been doing."

The woman didn't have a concept that she herself was still dreaming, so as Steve waved his hand to change scenery, the woman started getting angry when she saw her husband in the arms of another woman, and then she started crying.

"Is this how you want to live?" Steve asked without compassion.

"No," she mumbled between her cries.

"Then get your revenge," he said callously.

"*What?*" she asked, shocked.

"If you don't like what you see, then get your revenge and change it."

Looking toward the direction of Steve's voice, she saw her husband kissing the other woman, and then she started shouting and screaming, "Honey, don't!"

"Margaret. Margaret!" John Owen shouted, trying to wake up his wife.

She opened her eyes. "Get away from me. Get away from me!" she screamed and then ran from their bed to lock herself in the bathroom, where her husband could hear her cries. Trying to talk to her through the bathroom door, Mr. Owen pleaded with his wife to tell him what had upset her.

"You're having an affair with another woman!" she shouted.

"I am not!" he insisted. "What are you talking about?" He tried to explain to Mrs. Owen that she'd only had a dream.

Steve knew, however, that although it was just a dream, when Mrs. Owen saw her husband doing something she didn't like, it still affected her reality emotions, just as it affected her dream emotions. Not only did Steve subject Mrs. Owen to a nightmare, but he had also forced her to watch a dream that wasn't her husband's.

Steve woke up on the bed in the infirmary, not sure how he felt about what he'd just done. Any other time in the past when he would give someone a nightmare, it was because he wanted something. But now, Tillian had given him the order, and he felt somewhat regretful for what he'd done. Steve now sat in the interrogation room, alone and hooked up to the wires that led to the other side of the mirror, and he felt more alone than he ever had felt.

He was questioned about which powers he'd used, and about the woman's reaction—if she thought she was in reality or not. Over the next three or four days, Steve would continually give the same dream to the woman, until she gave in to her nightmare.

As I headed downstairs to leave for school, my dad sat in the living room, watching the morning news. I heard the newscaster say something about a local government official's wife who had been placed in psychiatric care after going on about someone in her dreams. I sat down on the couch, waiting for the newscast to continue after the commercial break, and a fear started coming over me.

"Since when are you interested in the news?" my dad chuckled.

Before I could answer, the newscaster continued her story.

"About four this morning, police were called out to Councilman Owen's home when neighbors heard gunshots coming from inside. When police arrived at the scene, they found Mr. Owen upstairs on the bedroom floor, bleeding from at least two gunshot wounds to the chest. Mrs. Owen, his wife, was sitting in the corner of their bedroom, crying, as a gun lay next to her on the floor. Mr. Owen was taken to Mercy Hospital, where he's in stable condition.

"Mrs. Owen has since been taken to an undisclosed location, where she is undergoing psychiatric evaluation. According to police reports, Mrs. Owen had attempted to kill her husband over a dream. Mrs. Owen said that someone has been showing her dreams inside her dreams of her husband cheating with another women. And these dreams have been recurring over the last few nights. We'll keep you posted as more information comes in on this bizarre case of cheating in dreams."

"Well, that's a new one on me," my dad said as he got up from his chair.

"Yeah, it is." I said softly, wondering if by chance I might have indirectly had a part in it.

The last few days, Bobby had been enjoying his own dreams. Even though we would talk and see each other, he wanted time to be alone in dreams. He didn't want any involvement with the police or Tillian, but it was he who was the first one to call about the newscast.

"Do you think it's Steve?" Bobby asked, as if reading my thoughts.

"It seems like it," I replied as I sat there feeling heartbroken, thinking of Mr. Owen being shot.

"Man, we've got to stop messing with other people's dreams," Bobby said, sounding troubled.

I wasn't sure if we could stop. Sure, we could stop going into other people's dreams, but even then, we would still be aware of our own dreams. Could we resist the temptation of letting dream control go?

"I need to contact Steve somehow," I said, letting Bobby know I couldn't just walk away. I'd started feeling everything was my fault. If Steve caused the woman to shoot her husband, then I was partially to blame and needed to ensure that it didn't happen again.

I then started thinking about the shadow I saw in Steve's dream the other night. If Steve wasn't the one who went into Mrs. Owen's dream, then who did? Call me egotistical, but up until that point, I hadn't thought it was possible for there to be more Luciders.

CHAPTER 8 DREAM ASSASSINS

When Steve was escorted to the interrogation room for his morning inquisition—where, for once, he wasn't strapped to the chair—he saw a newspaper that had been left behind by the guards. He recognized a newspaper photograph of a woman as the same woman he had been visiting in her dreams. As he read the newspaper report, he soon became queasy.

"I never thought it would be possible, but yet, I'm standing here, witnessing it for myself. Very well done," Tillian's voice said with excitement as he looked at Steve through the two-way mirror.

Steve sat in the chair, staring at the words "gunshot wounds to the chest" in the newspaper report until he was overcome with nausea, and he started vomiting on the floor. "You son of a bitch!" Steve shouted at Tillian. "I'm now an attempted murderer."

"How can you be an attempted murderer? It was only a dream, wasn't it?" Tillian said quietly. "And I must say, I had my doubts that you could do it. I commend you." He hid his smile behind the mirror.

"Go to hell!" Steve responded angrily.

Tillian ignored Steve's comments. "After a few more tests, I believe you'll be ready."

"I won't do it anymore," Steve insisted defiantly, heading for the door.

"The door's locked," Tillian said breezily. Then his tone turned harsh. "You agreed to this; now sit down."

"I'm not a murderer!" Steve shouted. He picked up the paper from the floor and threw it toward the mirror.

"No," Colonel Tillian told Steve.

"You weren't ever going to let me go, were you?" Steve finally said.

"No."

Steve ran up to the mirror, cussing and hitting it as hard as he could until the guards came. Steve fought the guards, but one of the guards used a taser gun on him, after which he was carried back to his cell. Tillian left the observation room and went back to his office, where he made a phone call confirming his own orders and preparing for Steve's next assignment.

Steve was put back into his cell to calm down, but he was later brought back into the interrogation room. This time, the guards strapped him in the chair and a nurse injected him with a drug.

"I hope you're feeling better, Mr. Holcomb," Colonel Tillian said from the other side of the mirror. The drug had taken effect, and Steve was barely able to answer. He tried his best to tell Tillian where he could go, but all he could do was sit there and listen. "Tonight, you'll have a new assignment. The photos will be in your room. Study them very carefully, and do not communicate with anyone. And remember," Tillian lied, "I do have someone watching you." Tillian watched Steve struggle to keep his head up. "Do you understand?" he asked. Not getting an answer, he repeated, "Do you understand?"

Steve nodded his head.

"Good. And I'm sure I don't need to explain what you're supposed to do."

Steve was taken to the infirmary, where he was kept sedated until he fell asleep later that night.

Detective Long walked into Dr. Maiden's office carrying a copy of the morning newspaper. "I'm assuming you've read this?"

"Yes, I've read it," Maiden replied.

"You don't seem too concerned."

"I'm concerned; I'm just not surprised," Maiden replied somewhat callously.

"So Tillian used Holcomb to do this, and you're just sitting there?" Mike Long said flatly.

"What the hell do you want me to do?" Maiden said harshly. "Tell the media Tillian used a boy's dream to have a councilman's wife have nightmares that eventually led her to shoot her husband? Mike, I warned you. That's why I told you what I did. But I'm not going to put my reputation on the line to clear the kid—it's just not going to happen. I'm sorry."

"So what do I do?" the detective asked Jerry Maiden.

"Nothing," Dr. Maiden plainly stated. Without blinking, he took a drink of his coffee while looking at Long. "Mike, as your friend, I'm telling you—if you try to find out what's going on, you'll be sitting in that same chair, not as a friend but as a patient."

"Are you threatening me?" Mike asked, standing up and raising his voice.

"No, Mike, the courts will find you guilty of insanity with your story. Why do you think I've kept my mouth shut all these years?" Dr. Maiden stood up and went around his desk to sit on the corner of it. Almost in a whisper, he said, "I warned you, not so you could find the truth, but so you could keep it hidden."

"Hidden? Why in hell would I do that?"

"The truth is, the other kids who have the same abilities as Holcomb are who you need to protect right now," Jerry said.

"Tillian," Detective long said and started to leave. But just as he was about to walk out the door, Maiden picked up the newspaper on his desk and said pointedly, "Mike, there will be more headlines like this one."

"The hell with you and your damn prophecy," Mike responded and walked out, slamming the door behind him.

Dr. Maiden stood there looking at the closed door, thinking that the first time he tried to stop what was happening he'd lost his job. Now, he wasn't trying to stop it, and he'd lost one of his good friends.

When I picked Rae up for school, I told her everything I had heard on TV.

"Don't you think we should contact Detective Long?" she said.

"What is he going to do?" I asked her, feeling irritated. "How is he going to help us?"

"Well, I don't think our parents are going to be able to help, do you?" Rae replied, feeling just as helpless as I did. "David, we need to do something. We can't just walk around town waiting for Tillian to pick us up."

"Pick us up?" I questioned, not understanding what she was referring to.

"Remember? Detective Long said Tillian might find out what he could about Steve, and then he might start looking for us."

I started feeling overwhelmed with fear, so much so that I immediately questioned every car coming in the parking lot and everyone walking by.

"Where the hell is Bobby? He said he'd meet us here!" I shouted loudly as I hit the steering wheel with my hand.

"I want to get out of here!" Rae said, clearly upset. "I have to think."

I started feeling the same as Rae—it was time we left, and Bobby would have to catch up to us later. But as soon as we started pulling out of our parking spot, I saw Sally trying to wave us down. I stopped the car, and Rae rolled down her window as Sally ran over to the passenger's side.

"Hey, where are you going? You'll be late for school," she said.

"I forgot about something. I'll be back later," Rae responded.

"Is everything okay?" Sally asked Rae, although she gave me a dirty look.

"Sally, let it go," I told her.

"Everything's fine," Rae confirmed.

Sally looked at Rae through narrowed eyes but then said, "Okay, I might as well give you this now." She handed Rae a note. "Bobby wanted me to give it to you when I saw you in class. He stopped by my house this morning."

"Bobby left a note for Rae?" I asked. "Not for me?"

"I guess he knows I don't like you," she responded with a sneer. "I'll see you later, Rae," Sally told her and left.

Rae tore open the note. All it said was "Don't use the phone, and head home."

"This doesn't make sense," I said. "I'm calling him."

"Don't," Rae said. "David, why would Bobby send this with Sally if something wasn't right?"

I had to admit, it wasn't like Bobby to act this way. I was feeling very worried now as to what was going on. "Maybe we should contact Detective Long," I suggested, as I put the car into drive and headed toward her house, and that's when I saw what I believed was the reason for Bobby's secrecy.

We reached Rae's street and drove by a suspicious-looking car near her house.

"David, you just passed my house," Rae told me, trying to get my attention.

"We're going somewhere else," I said as I kept driving.

She nodded as she saw me look in the rearview mirror, and she looked out the rear window trying to see if anyone was coming down the road. "I don't see anyone."

We didn't know if Tillian had someone watching us, but we weren't about to take that chance. We looked for someplace to hide, but after a few moments of driving, my phone rang, showing an unfamiliar number. I let it go to voicemail and got a message from Bobby, who told us to drive to Williams Street, take a right, and then pull over. As I turned on Williams Street, I saw the same car that had been parked by Rae's house. It pulled up next to us—but I felt relieved when the window rolled down, and I saw Bobby's face.

"Follow me to Tealo's apartment," he said.

Once we met at Tealo's, Bobby explained what had been happening. Earlier, he'd heard his grandma talking to someone from the police department. His grandma said the man had wanted to ask Bobby questions about Steve and a stolen car.

"Detective Long was correct," Rae said interrupting Bobby's story.

He then told us that his grandma had told the person at the door that Bobby had already left for school. He told us that he climbed over the fence into the neighbor's backyard and then headed to Sally's, hoping she hadn't left for school yet.

"But why are you using Tealo's car and phone? And why didn't you stop us when we passed you at Rae's?" I felt somewhat annoyed with the cat-and-mouse game we seemed to be playing.

"I left my own phone at home—that's why I said not to call. And I couldn't get to my car because they were still there when I went to Sally's. I didn't stop you at Rae's because I wanted to make sure you weren't being followed—that's why it took a few minutes for me to catch up to you guys." He took a deep breath and gave me a quizzical look, as if he couldn't understand why I wasn't able to figure it all out.

"And just think—he graduates in a month," Rae said, grinning.

"I'm glad someone thinks this is funny," I said, raising an eyebrow. I knew, though, that Rae was trying to make light of things to help us all feel better. We spent most of the day at Tealo's house, trying to figure out what we were going to do.

First, we had to let our parents know that we were staying with someone for a few days—we knew the police would ask them about us. Next, we had to find Steve. We thought if we could find Steve in dreams, then we just might be able to help him in reality.

As night once again came, we sat at Tealo's, trying to figure what we needed to do. Rae was in the spare bedroom, Bobby was in Tealo's bed (Tealo worked nights), and I fell asleep on the couch. I woke up at the pond, where Rae and Bobby also materialized. Before setting out to look for Steve, we tried once more to call him but without success. We even tried to contact Steve using visualization, but the portal to Steve seemed to be distorted, and we weren't able to appear into his dream.

We decided to split up and search for Steve. Rae said that she would go to Steve's house but needed me to open the gateway because she had never been there. When the portal was opened and his house came into view, she said, "Looks somewhat creepy." We discussed where Bobby and I would search, and Rae finally stepped through the gateway into the farm fields just in time to see a light extinguished next to the house.

Rae wasn't sure what the light was, so she decided against reappearing at the house. She called Steve's name thinking it might be him and startled Lieutenant Miller, who stood in front of Steve's house. Lieutenant Miller had seen and had gone through her own portal to Steve's house just before Rae got there. She then heard Rae shouting Steve's name. Not wanting to be spotted, she floated up a tree that stood at the corner of the house and hid in the branches.

Lifting herself up and floating around the farmlands and woods in the area, Rae tried to find anything that might be suspicious. She continued her search as she flew closer to the house. Reaching the house, Rae floated in front of the porch. "Steve?" she called as she looked all around the house. "Steve?" she said again and drifted back down toward the ground.

Waving her hand in front of her, the front door opened up. She floated down to the porch and walked in the house, into the living room, created some light to see. "Now I see what David was talking about," Rae said to herself when she saw the shrine of Sue above the fireplace surrounded by candles. Looking at the walls, she also saw the words "Help me" spelled out in black letters. And then, when she was heading back out the front door, Rae called to me in my dream. "David!"

Bobby and I appeared in front of Steve's house, where Rae sat on the steps of the porch, her head resting in her arms. "Rae?" I said. Looking up at Bobby and me, she stood up and walked back into the house.

We followed her inside, and she closed the door. Written on the back of the door was the word "Killers."

"Killers?" I said.

"Well, I guess he's found a way to communicate with us," Bobby spoke up.

"Yes, and to let us know what's going on," I responded.

"Rae, what's the matter?" Bobby questioned her when he noticed she was in deep thought.

"There's something I haven't been able to figure out," Rae finally said. "If Steve is coherent enough to leave a message, why can't we find him in his dreams? We know what he looks like, but when we visualize him, we can't get a good contact. When we call his name, he doesn't answer, but he comes to us asking for help. And finally, he comes here and leaves a message, but why doesn't he just stay here?"

We just didn't know what to think. What was making it so hard for us to find him? After agreeing to stay together and look some more before we had to wake up, Bobby created a doorway outside the house. Rae and I stepped through to other fields, but Bobby hesitated. After looking around the yard and out through the fields, he vanished into the gateway.

After we had left Steve's house, Lieutenant Miller instantly stood on the porch. "Who is keeping them from communicating with you?" Lieutenant Miller also questioned why we weren't able to get into Steve's dream. After walking into the house and eventually seeing what Steve wrote, she quickly vanished into another dream.

We floated above the farms, looking in different parts of dream world for any sign of Steve. Suddenly, the scenery changed. "Look at that," Bobby said as we drifted up to the clearing on the other side of the ridge. In the distance, we saw what seemed to be a fortress just beyond the river. It separated the open fields and hills, where we were, from the thick forest that hid the base of the fortification that rose above the trees.

We landed on the ground to get our bearings. "Rae?" I asked, thinking she was the one who'd changed the surrounding area without our knowledge.

"It's not my doing," she replied

"Look out!" Bobby shouted when balls of flame shot out from the city, exploding all around us as we got closer to the river. As we headed back in the opposite direction, an explosion knocked Rae and me in the air and Bobby to the ground.

Just as Bobby was about to hit the ground, we faded from sight.

"Son of a bitch!" I spoke. I sat up on the couch as Rae came out of the spare bedroom.

"David, that was too damn real for me," she said, shaken up by the explosions. "What was that all about?"

"I don't know," I said, and then I got up and knocked on the bedroom door where Bobby slept.

"How can he still be sleeping after all that?" Rae asked when we didn't get an answer. We entered the room and found Bobby was still sleeping … but not by his choice.

Lying on the ground, Bobby heard voices coming in his direction.

"Get up," a woman's voice said as he felt a kick to his side. "I said get up."

Being unaware of what was going on, Bobby looked up and saw a woman in shorts towering over him. The sun was shining on one side of her head, hiding her face.

"Bring him" were the last words Bobby heard from the woman just as he passed out. Floating a little above the grass, with no support holding him up, Bobby was stretched out on his back. His hands and feet were bound with streams of light made of energy, and then his captors took him away.

Regaining consciousness just as the group walked out of the thick forest on the other side of the river, Bobby looked around to see a few of his captors. The men wore black khaki pants that were rolled over at the top edge of their boots and sleeveless jean jackets with no shirts. The women in the group also wore black clothes, but they had on shorts, halter tops, and ankle boots.

"David! Rae!" Bobby started shouting.

"Shut up," the man who was walking next to him said, as Bobby was still floating above the ground.

"The hell with you man!" Bobby responded, struggling, trying to get free. "Man, you better let me go before I beat your ass!"

"I told you to shut up." The man touched Bobby's side with his hand, sending an electrical current into Bobby's body.

"You bastard!" Bobby screamed in agony, as the man chuckled.

Sandy, who was leading the group, wore a bandana around her head to keep her long red hair from getting in her face. She stopped walking to let the group catch up. As she approached Bobby and the man, Bobby saw she had a snake tattoo covering the length of the left side of her body; it weaved in and out of her clothes and areas of her body.

"James? Why the hell do you even argue with him?" Sandy questioned the man next to Bobby. Not waiting for a reply, Sandy pointed her finger in Bobby's direction, and a beam of rainbow light shot out from her finger, locking his mouth shut. She heard Bobby trying to speak, but he could only mumble. She led the group into the city.

Coming into the city, Bobby saw more of his captors, who were dressed the same as the ones bringing him in. The group stopped in the middle of the courtyard, where they stood in front of the leader of the compound. Carson wore the same sleeveless black jean jacket as the others, but his was open, revealing a tattoo on his muscular chest.

The tattoo was of two snakes coiling up and forming an X with their bodies, while their heads faced each other, as if each was ready to strike the other. On the back of his jacket were the words, in red, "Even in your dreams, I'll find you." On his cowboy hat, from which long hair sprouted, was the same snake picture as his tattoo. He wore dark sunglasses and had a full beard, so Bobby was unable to determine what Carson looked like.

"He's trying to free himself with his mind," Sandy told Carson as he watched Bobby struggling to get free.

"Dream powers?" Carson looked at Bobby, perplexed. "Are you sure?" Carson chuckled at Bobby, who was still floating above the ground in a prone position. "Let him stand up," Carson said, turning his back to Bobby as he lit a cigarette. Sandy waved her hand toward Bobby and the invisible force that held him up gave way, causing him fall about three feet to the ground. She then released the bands of light from his legs so that he could stand up.

Carson stood there, his back still toward Bobby, listening to the grumbling sounds Bobby was making. "Sandy put a force around you, preventing you from using any dream sorcery you might have," he said. "And the way she was able to subdue you quickly, I'd say you're somewhat of a new person in dreams."

"You want me to release him?" Sandy asked as she walked over to Bobby and ran her index fingernail down his cheek and across his chin, stopping on his lips as she smiled at Bobby.

"What do you think?" Carson asked Bobby as he finally turned to look at him. "Shall we release you so that we can hear what you have to say?" He nodded to Sandy.

"Bitch," Bobby said once Sandy released the spell she had over his mouth.

"Yeah, I've heard it before." She smiled and blew Bobby a kiss with the finger she'd used on his lips as she walked away.

"I got your kiss. Release my hands, and I'll show you what I can do with my finger," Bobby spat at Sandy.

Sandy again prevented him from talking, and Carson walked over and blew smoke into Bobby's face. "As long as you're going to keep running your big mouth, she's going to shut it for you. You understand?" Carson asked Bobby and blew smoke again in his face.

Bobby nodded his head, and Sandy released the spell again. "What? No kiss this time?" he said. When he saw Sandy's finger pointing at him, he quickly said, "Okay. Okay."

"You're thick as hell, aren't you, kid?" Carson said, smiling at Bobby.

Bobby looked around and saw other men and women standing in the courtyard. Each of them also had some representation of a snake, either on their outfits or as tattoos. Some were hiding their faces with scarves and sunglasses, while others weren't wearing anything over their faces. "What have you done with my friends?" Bobby asked.

"We didn't do anything with your friends," Carson replied.

"They were with me when your assholes started firing on us," Bobby said, still struggling to get the electric stream handcuffs loose.

"I assure you, we haven't done anything with them. And besides, I'm pretty sure I'm the one here who's going to be asking questions," Carson said arrogantly as he walked around Bobby.

"Why are you here?" Carson asked, coming back around in front of Bobby.

"Here? Where's here?" Bobby looked around the courtyard in the middle of the city.

"We know you have the capabilities of understanding dreams. How do you think Sandy was able to tell us you were trying to use dream sorcery to escape?" Carson said, ignoring Bobby's question. "So, once again I ask: why are you here?"

"Where the hell are my friends?" Bobby replied angrily.

"I see we're not getting anywhere right now." Carson walked away from Bobby and pointed his hand toward Sandy to take over.

"Man, look, I just want to know where my friends are," Bobby said quickly, wondering what Carson was going to have Sandy do next.

"I'm assuming that after the blast, they woke from their dream," Carson replied. "Yes, I know you understand what I'm talking about."

Bobby understood what Carson was referring to. "Why didn't I wake up?" Bobby questioned, confused.

"I'm not sure," Carson replied, pulling on his beard.

"That was me," Lieutenant Miller said.

Carson looked over at Lieutenant Miller in confusion. "Regardless," Carson said. "I assure you we didn't want you around here and would have preferred that you woke up, too."

"Shit, man, apparently you know we're dreaming. It's just a dream. What does it matter if I'm here or not?" Bobby asked, chuckling a little.

Carson's expression changed from complacent to concerned. He spoke louder and harsher to Bobby.

"Just a dream? No, we're not just in a dream. We're in reality. Our reality!" Carson spread his arms, pointing to his companions.

"Can we just get rid of him?" Sandy asked Carson, walking toward Bobby and moving her fingers around.

Bobby smiled at Sandy. "Honey, even with your half-snake body, you're a fine-looking lady. But you need to change your attitude if you gonna get anyone like me."

Just as Sandy lifted her finger toward Bobby again, Carson said, "Enough! I want answers, and I want them *now*." He narrowed his eyes as he looked at Bobby. "Who are you?" When Bobby didn't immediately answer, Carson walked away, saying, "James."

James walked over to Bobby and smiled, and then he touched Bobby's side with his hand again. He laughed as Bobby screamed from the electrical shock and then fell to the ground.

"Captain!" Lieutenant Miller said in shock, watching James torment Bobby.

"Now … answer my questions!" Carson said, raising his voice, ignoring the lieutenant.

"Go to hell!" Bobby said defiantly.

"As I said, you're thick as hell. But we have all the time in the world."

After a few more shocks from James, Lieutenant Miller once again spoke up. "Sir, you have got to stop this."

Bobby was hurting from the shocks he was receiving and began sharing information with Carson.

Carson didn't pay too much attention to Bobby until he talked about Colonel Tillian. "*What* did you say?"

"Shit! He's waking!" Sandy said as Bobby started to fade from view.

"Stop him!" Carson shouted.

"I can't! He's naturally waking up!" Sandy responded.

Carson turned to Miller. "You want to tell me what's going on?"

"Captain, right now I can't. Please believe me," Lieutenant Miller said and then vanished into Steve's dream.

Steve stood in the banquet hall where he saw Senator Wilson dreaming of hundreds of people sitting around tables in honor of his birthday. They were eating, drinking, laughing, and dancing to the music, and he thought about what he was going to do. Suddenly, the guests started screaming as the floor beneath them starting shaking.

Floating above the screaming crowd that was panicking and trying to run out of the banquet hall, Steve landed in front of Senator Wilson, preventing him from waking up. Immediately, they both stood on a summit of a mountain, in front of a fire pit. "You're the one who's trying to stop the project," Steve spoke to the fearful senator.

"What project?" the dreamer questioned, not understanding his new dream.

"Dream Catcher. You're the one who's fighting the funding," Steve spoke again. "And until you change your mind, you'll learn how it feels by not having this project."

Wilson instantly hovered over the fire pit. "What are you doing? Change my mind about what?" Wilson questioned in fear as the flames grew a little at a time, tormenting him.

"Dream Catcher is not to be shut down!" Steve shouted above the senator's screams, as small energy balls flew from Steve's hand, shocking Wilson.

Miller shouted toward Steve, "Holcomb, stop!" Metal spikes in the ground started moving upward, piercing Wilson's body, as he lay there, unable to move, screaming for his life.

Steve looked toward Julie. "Who are you?" he asked.

"Please, let him go," she said.

Letting the spikes continue, fire came out of Steve's eyes. It just missed Lieutenant Miller, as she faded and then reappeared behind Steve.

"You don't want to do this," she told him. "Let him wake up."

Steve ignored her request. Lightning bolts shot from Steve's hands, only to be blocked by a force field around the lieutenant.

"Mr. Holcomb!" Julie shouted. Then she spoke more sensitively. "Steve ... I don't want to fight you. I'm here to help."

"Damn it! Now he's waking up!" Steve shouted angrily at Lieutenant Miller as he watched Senator Wilson wake up naturally. He sent countless colored energy balls toward the lieutenant, knocking her on the ground.

Appearing behind Steve, Captain Carson used an electrical stream from his hand that generated enough force to send Steve flying in the air and land some distance away.

"Captain, don't!" the lieutenant shouted as Captain Carson raised his hands up.

But with the humming of the energy ball, Captain Carson didn't hear her in time. The energy from his hands grew larger and faster, heading toward Steve and encasing him in the sphere of electricity that prevented him from using any dream sorcery.

Lieutenant Miller walked over to the sphere where Steve was frantically trying to escape. "Captain, please release him," she requested.

"Lieutenant, are you out of your mind?" Captain Carson questioned.

"Please, sir," she asked, sympathetic to Steve.

As soon as Captain Carson released Steve from the energy sphere, Steve stood with Julie in front of his house. She said, "I really can help you." Steve then faded ... and woke up in the infirmary.

When Bobby had woken up, he sat up in the bed, feeling the area where James had tortured him. "We have problems!" he said, walking out of the bedroom.

"What?" I questioned.

"There are others just like us," Bobby said, staring at us. "There were about a dozen in the city. They also have powers, and from what I can tell, they're very good at using them." He rubbed his side.

"More than ours?" I asked.

Bobby nodded. "At least from what I was able to feel of it." He then told us what they had done to him. "It's like they've been lucid dreamers for a very long time," he said.

Rae spoke up. "It must have been one of those people who you thought you saw in Steve's dream."

We all just sat there for a moment, wondering who these people were and why they'd wanted to make Bobby suffer.

"One more thing," Bobby said. "When I mention Tillian, Carson seemed interested."

CHAPTER 9 LUCIDERS

Bobby had been in the presence of many Luciders—people who were aware that they were dreaming inside a dream—and he'd felt their gifts firsthand. Those he'd just left were more than just lucid dreamers, though; they were organized and very quick at what they did, not leaving anything for chance.

We sat at the kitchen table, eating breakfast and discussed what Bobby had discovered—or should I say, what had discovered him. "I knew I should have stayed in my own dreams," Bobby said, verbalizing the thoughts each of us shared.

"Why haven't we come across them before?" Rae asked.

"Maybe we have but just didn't notice?" I suggested.

"What do you mean?" Rae asked, looking confused.

I remembered the shadow in Steve's dream and also started thinking that the Luciders could have been hiding in plain sight all this time.

"In our dreams, we create our surroundings and dreamers, but we also have come across dreams where dreamers appear and disappear without our influence," I explained.

"These Luciders—could they have been one or more of those dreamers, watching us without our knowledge?" Rae asked.

Even though I didn't answer, Bobby and Rae both knew that was what I was starting to believe.

"Do you think they're working for Tillian?" Rae questioned, even though it seemed certain that they were.

"It's just a guess, but I'd say yes," I answered. "They could have been the ones who were preventing us from contacting Steve somehow."

"On the other hand," Bobby said, "the Luciders were adamant about wanting to know who we were and what were we doing there. So if they were working for Tillian, they were left in the dark about us. But if they weren't working for Tillian, then who are they working for?" Bobby stared at us.

"Maybe they were just lucid dreamers who had organized themselves in dream world," Rae said.

"Either way, they're a link we found to Tillian in our dreams," I replied.

We agreed the best plan for us was to stay where we were. But soon, my phone and Rae's started ringing. I let it go to my voicemail. When I checked my voicemail, I found there were numerous messages from my dad and mom, telling me to come home and asking me what was going on because the police had come by, asking questions about Steve. Rae also had a text message from Mary. Mary needed to see Rae in their dreams tonight.

I knew my parents would be at work and Tommy and Wendy would be at school, so I called and left a message on the house phone. I let my parents know that I was okay and what they might have heard from the cops was not entirely true. I told them that I was not involved with Steve stealing the car, but I didn't think the cops would believe me. However, I did lie when I told them that I believed I knew who that person was, and I was getting help from someone to prove Steve's innocence.

I lied to them out of desperation—how could I explain to my mom and dad what I was capable of doing or that a U.S. military colonel might be trying to find me. I wasn't willing to be admitted into Lifelong. My lying to them wasn't just for my own benefit. But the truth of the matter was that if we were going to prove ourselves innocent of whatever we'd been accused, I needed to find the person that Bobby said was named Carson and figure out what his role in dream world was.

"David, I don't think we should be confronting those bastards," Bobby said after I explained that we needed to talk with the other Luciders.

"But if they have the key to all of this, we need to try. If not for ourselves, then for Steve," I insisted. "At least open the gateway to where they are." I hoped he would change his mind about going to see Carson with me.

I could tell Bobby was reluctant to go back into their dream city by the way he kept rubbing his side—he didn't want to go back and have more of their treatment. I did eventually persuade him to open the portal for me, but I couldn't persuade him to go with me that night to meet Carson and his thugs.

"We've overlooked one thing," Rae said. "Who changed our dream?"

Bobby thought a moment. "There was a woman there who told Carson she had brought us there."

"Who?" I asked.

"I'm not sure. But Carson seemed confused as to why she would bring us into their dream." He closed his eyes, trying to remember everything.

"Did you get a look at her? Maybe she's the one we need to find," Rae said.

Bobby shook his head. "No, she was just another face among many—although I couldn't really see her face clearly. Carson was blocking my view."

"That's too bad," I said, thinking out loud. "If Carson wasn't expecting us, then it has to be that woman who knows what's going on. She must have wanted us there for a reason."

Steve had questions of his own he needed answered, but when he was taken to the interrogation room for his morning inquiry from Tillian after his dream data was analyzed, he wasn't sure how to ask. He met two Luciders, but he didn't know if they were the ones following him or even if they worked for Tillian.

"It seems you had a rough night," Colonel Tillian said.

"What do you mean?" Steve asked innocently.

"It seems that just prior to your waking up, your brain activity increased tremendously. You want to talk about what happened?" Tillian asked.

Steve looked toward the mirror and tried to appear confused. "I can't remember," he said quietly.

Tillian looked down at Lieutenant Mitchell, who was monitoring Steve's polygraph and confirmed that Steve was telling the truth.

"Start from the beginning," Tillian instructed him. Each time Steve explained what had happened and what he'd done to Senator Wilson, the lieutenant reconfirmed the story. But Steve couldn't account for the time after the fireballs and the shocking of Wilson. And it was at this point in Steve's dream that the monitors showed Steve's brain activity increased.

Tillian picked up the phone in the observation room. "Wake Lieutenant Miller," he told the person on the other end.

In the infirmary, in the room next to where Steve would dream, a nurse brought Miller out of her sleep. She was groggy from being awakened. "How long?" the lieutenant asked the nurse next to her bed.

"A few days, ma'am," the nurse replied.

Miller sat on the bed, drinking some water and trying to get stable after lying in bed. She went back to her room to make herself presentable before reporting to Tillian, as ordered. She wondered if Tillian had her awake because of Steve.

"Good afternoon, sir," Julie said as she entered his office.

"How are you feeling?" he asked.

"Fine, sir," the lieutenant said. "Sir, the nurse said I was only asleep for a few days. Is everything okay? I'm curious as to why I was woken early."

"Holcomb can't seem to remember the last part of his dream," Tillian told her. "Are you certain Birch hasn't been in contact with Holcomb?"

Julie shook her head. "Not possible, sir. I've been keeping watch on his friends, and even though they were calling for Holcomb, they never made dream contact."

"Okay, Lieutenant. That'll be all. Thank you."

"Sir, if I may … it's been over three months, and I really could use a few days off to see my boys."

Tillian nodded and granted Miller a few days of relaxation. "But I want you to continue checking on Birch," he added.

"Yes, sir," the lieutenant said and then left the colonel's office.

I need to have them brought in, Tillian thought. "Something's going on," he said out loud. And he then called for his car to take him to the airport, leaving instructions for Steve to be heavily sedated until he returned.

On her way to visit her children, Lieutenant Milled made a detour.

She pulled up to a location deep in the woods. It was isolated from everyone and everything. She stopped her car in front of a gate where two heavily armed soldiers stood guard. Another guard came up behind the car, using mirrors to view underneath and a dog to sniff the area. And still another guard came from inside the guard shack, demanding her identification, and then radioed to the house.

"Captain Carson wants you to head straight for the briefing room," the guard said and then handed her identification back.

The gates opened up, allowing Lieutenant Miller to pass through. As she drove down the long road, she saw more soldiers observing her as she drove. Upon reaching the location of the house, she was permitted to pass another gate without being stopped. She was greeted by more guards as she pulled up in front of the house. She handed one the keys to her car, along with all of her belongs. Then she was escorted through a number of detectors and into the living room of the house.

"This way, Lieutenant," a master sergeant said, pointing his hand in the direction she was to go. She walked through a door on the other side of the living room; it led to an elevator that went underground, where she went into a briefing room. She saw Captain Carson sitting at the table. He was clean-shaven, with short hair, and wearing his military uniform.

"Captain," Lieutenant Miller said.

"Lieutenant," the captain replied.

"The prodigal child has come back home," a voice from behind her said.

Julie turned around. "Lieutenant Sandy Waters," Julie said, smiling.

Others followed Sandy into the room. None of them looked like they did in their dreams.

After everyone was sitting down around the conference room table, Captain Carson spoke, "Okay, Lieutenant, why are we meeting here instead of in our dreams? And why did you reveal our dream location to the kids?"

"Sir, you'll understand the reason we are meeting here after I tell you why I brought the kids to our location," Julie responded. "There are four of them, and each one is capable of controlling dreams."

Captain Carson, along with others in the room, looked surprised by Lieutenant Miller words. "How do you know this, Lieutenant?" Captain Carson asked.

"The boy you saw with me is Steve Holcomb," the lieutenant said. "He's in custody, and I'm to verify that he has the ability to control dreams."

"Custody?" Lieutenant Sandy Waters asked.

"I'm not at liberty to discuss that at the moment," Lieutenant Miller said.

"So the kid who was fighting with you in the dream isn't a normal dreamer?" Captain Carson asked.

Julie shook her head. "Also, I continued to monitor Holcomb and his friends to learn what they are doing. I've discovered they are capable of controlling reality—at least, Holcomb can."

Sandy shook her head. "Julie, no one has the capability to control reality by dreams."

Lieutenant Miller told them about the news article she'd found in the paper regarding Councilman Owen. She also informed them of Steve's foster parents who were institutionalized because of dreams. "And that's why I believe Holcomb can control reality," Lieutenant Miller said. "Captain, after I left you, when the other kid you were interrogating woke up, I went into Holcomb's dream. He was in Senator Wilson's dream, tormenting him about keeping Dream Catcher alive." She watched everyone's expressions.

"How does he know about Dream Catcher?" the captain asked.

"Sir, these kids don't know what's going on," Julie said sternly. "They just happened to be caught up in dreams. However, I believe they can help us."

"Help us? In what way?" Lieutenant James asked.

Lieutenant Waters spoke up. "We've been learning dream control for a few years now. If these kids have the capability, as Julie says they do, then we will be able to learn from them." She turned to Lieutenant Miller for acknowledgment. "And that's why you brought the kid to us in dreams."

"Yes," Lieutenant Miller said. "Also, I'm worried that if I'm correct, Senator Wilson is in danger."

"Lieutenant Miller," Captain Carson said, "the something else that's going on that you're not able to discuss right now, does that have to do with a Colonel Tillian?"

Julie nodded her head.

"Very well," the captain said. "The one named Bobby—if I remember his name correctly—is the only one we've seen, we'll start with him in dreams. Lieutenant Miller, you continue to watch Holcomb."

"I haven't been able to get inside his dream since Wilson's dream. I don't know if he's blocking me or if someone else is." Julie sighed. "However, I can help with the others."

"Good. We also need to find out where these kids live, because if we don't get to them first, I believe this Colonel Tillian will. And they're going to be in the same situation as the Holcomb kid," said Captain Carson.

Captain Carson gave his team their assignments. "I don't need to tell you how important this is," Carson said. "You are not to make contact with any of these kids. You are only to track them in dreams until we can find them in reality."

While Lieutenant Miller was discussing Steve with Captain Carson, Colonel Tillian was meeting FBI agent Collins at the small airport outside of town.

"Colonel, how are you doing?" Agent Collins asked his ex-commander when he picked him up at the airport.

"Agent Collins," the colonel replied and shook his hand. "Did my message make any sense at all?"

"Yes, sir. I assigned a man to go look for the kids," Collins replied.

"I do appreciate this," Tillian said with a smile.

"Understood, sir. It's no problem. You said Holcomb was picked up originally for stealing a car. We can bring the others in as accomplices," Collins replied, also smiling.

That night we had our own assignments. Rae was going to contact Mary to find out what she wanted, and then she was going to team up with Bobby, who was going to keep searching for Steve, while I went to find Carson and—I hoped—the woman who brought Bobby to their city.

Rae fell asleep. She called Mary a couple of times, and then suddenly, Rae saw a house coming into focus. Stepping through the portal, Rae stood on the sidewalk next to the white fence that surrounded Mary's house. She felt the warmth of the sun on her face. Looking up at the house, Rae saw multicolored flowers in the window boxes that lined the front and side of the house. The shutters were painted a very light pink and stood out against the white background of the house. There were garden beds throughout the plush grass of the yard.

"Wow," Rae said as she looked at Mary's dream home. Rae had never seen the dream house Mary created for herself. They usually spent their time together creating new dream worlds, looking for exciting things to do, or spending dreams with their mom and dad. And it was their dad who Mary wanted to talk to Rae about.

"I've been trying to get a hold of you," Mary told Rae as she stepped out onto the porch.

"We weren't answering our phones," Rae said in her defense.

"First there were regular police, and then there was a detective, and now the FBI?" Mary said.

"I don't want you involved, Mary," Rae said, and then she patted her sister's hand.

"What did you want to see me about?"

"Dad's really depressed," Mary said sadly. "He doesn't need this right now, Rae."

"I know. But until we figure out what's going on, I can't come home. You remember Steve Holcomb?" Rae asked. When Mary nodded, Rae continued. "He is in trouble for something he was coerced into doing, and we're trying to help him."

Mary seemed to accept that explanation. Then she said, "I need you to see inside of Dad's dreams. I've tried to help him, but I don't know what to do."

Rae knew it was hard for her dad to cope, and she had been fighting within herself on whether or not she should use her father's dreams to change his reality. She was hoping that by visiting him in his dreams, he would come out of his depression. But he was still struggling with the loss of his wife, and now his daughter was on the run.

Rae stood in the shadow of the hallway, looking into the living room, watching her dad. He was sitting on the couch, staring at a picture of Mrs. Woods. "I love you and miss you," Rae heard him say to the picture while wiping the tear from his eye. Moving behind the couch, Rae bent over and gave her dad a hug. "I love you, Daddy," she said and then kissed him on the cheek.

"I love you, too, sweetie," he replied with a forced smile. "Where's Mary?" Mr. Woods spoke to Rae as if he believed this was reality.

"She's around."

"We don't get to talk much lately," he said as he looked at the picture.

"No, and that's why I'm here." Rae walked around to the front of the couch and took the picture out of her dad's hands. "We all miss Mom very much," Rae said.

"You look as if you have something serious on your mind," he said, reaching for her hands.

"Dad, Mary and I need you," she began, and then Mary appeared and sat down next to them.

"I know you do," he responded. "Sometimes I try to talk to you, but as I start out, I lose the words I was going to tell you."

"Dad, please listen ..." Rae said. "Ever since Mom died, you've been getting farther away from us. We don't do the things we used to do as a family." She looked at another picture of all four of them that stood on the coffee table. "Daddy, we can't live like this anymore, and you can't live as if you don't exist. It's destroying all of us." Rae tried to hold back her tears.

"It's hard. There are days I wake up and tell myself things will be much better," he said quietly, staring at the floor. "But the more I try, the harder it gets for me to just get out of bed. I can't let her go." He now wept heavily as both daughters hugged him.

"Daddy," Mary spoke up, "you don't have to let Mom go. She's with us always, but we need to understand we have to continue living." Mary remembered how she felt at her mom's gravesite in her dream. "We need you now, more than ever before," she whispered.

"She's right, Daddy," Rae said. "We need to know that regardless of where you are, we can always count on you." Then she let him cry himself awake.

When Mr. Woods faded from his daughters, leaving them in the dream with tears in their eyes, Rae decided at that moment that she was going to use her gifts for something good, and she was going to start with her father.

After hugging her sister, as she never had, Rae gave Mary a kiss on her forehead and then called Bobby's name … and then she faded.

And just as Mary vanished from view, Lieutenant Sandy Waters walked out of the shadow of the dream, picked up the photo Mr. Woods was looking at, took a deep breath, and continued to follow Rae into Bobby's dream.

"Are you okay?" Bobby asked when Rae suddenly appeared through the gateway to his dream.

"Yes, I'm fine," she told him as she sniffled a little. "So where to?"

They stood there on a city sidewalk, watching dreamers walk around. "I figure this is just as good a place as any," Bobby responded. Bobby and Rae floated above the streets, calling Steve's name and visualizing his face, hoping to get a better connection to his dream.

"What if he doesn't want to be found?" Rae asked Bobby as they flew above the trees in the park.

He looked at her oddly. "Why do you think that?"

"Well, for almost two months now, since he was taken, we've only seen or heard from him once in a while. I'm just starting to believe he doesn't want to be found."

"If that's the case, why did he leave a message on the door?" Bobby asked.

Rae shrugged and said quietly, "I don't know. His life wasn't all that great in reality. Maybe he found something in dreams that he enjoys."

"I can't believe he would enjoy hurting people, Rae," Bobby said, trying to defend Steve's actions.

"Well, I'm starting to get tired of searching, only to find nothing."

"Rae, what are you getting at?" Bobby stared at her as they started floating to a bench just outside the park.

"I guess I'm just thinking of my dad," Rae said softly. "And if Steve doesn't want our help, we need to move on with our own dreams and the dreams of our family, to help them live better lives. That's all I'm saying." Rae spoke with sincerity, believing Steve had reached the point of not wanting to be found.

"Rae, we've been friends a long time. If you want to stop searching for Steve, I'm not going to fault you. And I don't believe David would either. David feels bad for getting Steve into this mess, and he wants to try to help Steve if he can." Bobby looked around at the dreamers. "I think David is right."

"What?" Rae questioned.

"We have company," Bobby whispered.

"Who?" Rae stood up and looked around.

Instead of telling Rae, Bobby walked over to a dreamer who was standing at the corner, waiting for the light to change. Waving his arm in front of the man just as he was about to walk, Bobby caused the dreamer to be immobile.

"Bobby, what are you doing?" Rae asked, confused.

"Help me, Rae. Do something in your mind at a dreamer, but don't say it out loud."

"Are you going insane?" she asked him with a slight chuckle.

Bobby walked back over to Rae, close enough so no one else could hear him. "See the dreamer sitting on the bench across the street from us?"

She looked past his shoulders. "What bench?"

"Shit!" Bobby said, after turning around and no longer seeing the bench. "Rae, I'm telling you. When we were sitting here, the bench faded into view. And the son of a bitch that was sitting on it—I believe he was that bastard who shocked the hell out of me when I ran into Carson and his gang."

As Rae looked harder in the direction where the bench had been, she chanted some words, and then a lightning bolt shot out from her hand, knocking Bobby on the ground as it passed him. It exploded just where the bench came back into view. "It's a portal!" Rae shouted at Bobby as she ran over to it.

Bobby started to get up from the ground, but a stream of energy came from the bench area, hitting Rae back toward the park. "Rae, are you okay?" Bobby shouted.

"Get that bastard before he leaves!" Rae shouted.

"Well, I'll be damned" Bobby said. James stood where the bench was. "Now I get to pay you back, you son of a bitch!" Bobby shouted, and lightning came from the sky, striking where James had stood only a second ago. "What the hell are you hiding for?" Bobby shouted into streets, trying to get James to show himself again.

"Bobby, look out!" Rae shouted at him as a blue light came

from her eyes, creating a shield that prevented a fireball from hitting Bobby.

"Thanks," Bobby said as he turned to Rae and smiled. Smiling back, Rae raised a hand up, creating a small whirlwind, blowing everything around in its path. Bobby headed in the direction of the fireball, which smashed into a small building, knocking out windows and doors. Dreamers were running everywhere. Some were disappearing as they woke from their own dreams, saying that they'd dreamed of a tornado. And other dreamers were waking into their dreams, only to be caught in the middle of the fight.

"I'm waiting!" Bobby shouted.

"Stop that!" Rae shouted at Bobby for instigating more trouble.

"I owe him," Bobby replied heatedly.

"Are you sure it's the same person?" Rae questioned him.

He turned around to answer her. "Oh yeah. That's the same ass," Bobby said when he saw James standing in the middle of the street, facing Bobby.

"I'm sorry about what happened before," James said, trying not to fight with Bobby, since he wasn't supposed to be seen.

"Sorry! Your ass is gonna be sorry in a minute!" Bobby shouted at him, and then a car lifted off the ground heading for James, who raised his hands up, causing a strong wind to blow the car into another vehicle. As Bobby and James kept tossing vehicles, lightning bolts, and even fire at one another, Rae floated in the air and started hurling boulders that seemed to appear right behind her. They headed toward James, smashing into the ground around him.

One of the boulders that appeared behind Rae turned into a fireball, knocking her aside. "That was my boulder," she said calmly, still able to hover. As James started to rise above the ground, the skies started getting dark, and lightning bolts shot out from the clouds all around Bobby and Rae, eventually knocking Rae to the ground. "Shit," she said after picking herself up and running for cover. The bolts starting splitting into smaller lightning strikes, spreading around the area.

Bobby continued to thrust his own energy in streams of different colored lights. James was hit by one of them and was thrown into a window of a building and then faded. Trying to catch his breath, Bobby continued looking at the window, waiting for James to show himself. Rae walked over next to him.

"Well done!"

Bobby and Rae both heard the woman's voice and turned to see Sandy sitting on a bench. "If you want to know about Mr. Holcomb, don't do it," Sandy said as both Rae and Bobby started raising their hands.

Both of them were exhausted from their fight with James. Hearing Sandy say Steve's name, they lowered their hands, still trying to catch their breath. Sandy faded from view, just as they woke up from the dream, still feeling tired and sweaty. Rae suddenly ran out of the bedroom into the living room.

"What happened?" I asked Rae as I sat on the couch.

"Where's Bobby?" she quickly asked.

"He's still asleep, I guess," I told her, wondering what was going on. And then Tealo's bedroom door opened and Bobby walked out, looking as if he'd just lost five fights.

"Look at you," I told him as he stumbled by.

Bobby ignored my comment. "Are you okay?" he asked Rae as he flopped down on a chair. As I looked at him and Rae, they both started laughing. Bobby said, "We kicked his ass, didn't we?"

"We sure did, buddy," Rae said and sat down next to me, giving me a morning kiss and hug.

"Did you have any luck?" Bobby asked me, trying to sit

upright.

"No. After you opened the gateway for me, I couldn't find the city on the other side of the river. It was all woods." I was still trying to figure out what was going on as I looked at both of them. "Now, what's with you two?"

"See, Rae?" Bobby said as he stood up. "Even if you want to stop looking for Steve, they can still find us."

"Remind me to practice the ability to not let anyone find me," she responded.

"I'm making coffee. You tell him what happened," Bobby said and left the room.

Rae proceeded to tell me everything that had happened in their dream.

"So they know where Steve is, then," I said after Rae finished telling me their encounter.

"Not sure," Rae responded.

"Great, now we have people looking for us in reality and in dreams," I said after Bobby brought us coffee.

"Yep," Bobby replied.

We spent the next few days hiding at Tealo's in reality and watching for Carson's group in dreams. After a while we were worried about being caught together and decided to split up and hide in different locations, while keeping contact in dreams. We were hoping that the search for us, at least in reality, was over, but we weren't sure until we tried to meet up at the pond.

After not being able to find us at our homes, Tillian left Collins in charge to continue the search for us while he went back home. When he got back to the facility where Steve was being held, Tillian was more frustrated at Steve's lack of progress with Senator Wilson. "You have been working for over a week on your assignment, and I haven't seen any results. Your sleep data is showing your dream state isn't even active. I've warned your ass—if you don't comply, you'll be stuck in your damn dreams. Why the hell aren't you getting into Wilson's dream?" Tillian shouted from the other side of the mirror at Steve.

"I've been trying. But when I get a glimpse of his dream, the gateway closes up before it comes completely into view, preventing me from seeing further into his dream!" Steve shouted angrily back at Tillian.

"I don't think you're trying as hard as you led me to believe. In fact, I think you've stopped searching all together," the colonel said.

"Sir, he's telling the truth," Lieutenant Mitchell said as she observed the needle movement on the machine.

"I keep telling you I can't reach his dream!" Steve said again. "I'm sensing someone else is around Wilson's dream, but I'm not able to see who it is."

"Your friends?" Tillian said more calmly.

"I don't think so. I've been preventing them from contacting me." Steve spoke as if he'd finally decided to be on Tillian's side.

Tillian thought about Steve's comment and then said, "Find a way to get through."

"I could concentrate a lot better if I wasn't drugged up so damn much," Steve said defensively.

Colonel Tillian thought back to a discussion he'd had with Jerry Maiden regarding the use of drugs and how they might interfere with test subject's ability to concentrate. Tillian also thought about how he had ordered some of his own troops to be isolated and how they were hidden because of what happened to them under the influence of some of the drugs they were given during the testing phase of the project. Tillian had so many drugs injected into Steve to get him to relax and dream that they also started leaving him incoherent inside of dreams. In addition, Steve's mental ability was being affected. Steve was starting to enjoy what he was doing for Tillian.

That night, having some compassion for Steve, Tillian

decided to let Steve stay in his room for the night instead of going to the infirmary to get drugged up. He believed Steve was unable to comprehend his dreams and needed regular rest. And that's when Steve turned on me.

I was on my way to the pond to meet Rae and Bobby. As I was about to cross the intersection, about a mile from the park, Rae called me. "Hurry—something is wrong."

"I should be there—"

"David?" Rae said into the phone. "David!" she shouted louder when I gave no response. "David!' Rae screamed into the phone. "We're cut off," she told Bobby worriedly.

"Rae, we need to get out of here now. Look!" Bobby said as he saw headlights in the dark coming through the park, heading toward the pond. They ran around the pond and down the train tracks that led into the woods and made their way toward Rae's house.

"Here!" Bobby said when he saw a vacant house in Rae's housing division. They ran around back and tried to find an unlocked door but weren't able to. Bobby grabbed a brick he pulled from the garden area in the backyard, tossed it into the small back-door window, put his hand through, and unlocked the door. "Hurry before anyone sees us," he told Rae as he held the door open for her.

Bobby went into the living room and peeked out the windows while Rae continued looking out the kitchen window to ensure no one had followed them. "I think we should be able to hide in here, at least for a day or two," Bobby told Rae after searching the upstairs of the house.

"I keep getting David's voice mail," Rae said after numerous times trying to call.

Finally falling asleep, Rae and Bobby stood at the pond. Just as they were about to leave through a portal, Bobby said, "Oh, hell no." Bobby realized that Sandy and James were materializing, as well as others he'd met in the city, and were now standing in front of him and Rae.

"We're not here to fight," Carson said as Bobby and Rae took a defensive position.

"No?" Rae said in disbelief, still holding the energy ball in her hand.

"No. We're not," Lieutenant Miller said as she walked from behind Carson.

"You!" Bobby recognized that she was the one who had changed the dream scenery when Bobby first met Carson.

"Hello again, Mr. Eriks," Julie said softly, and she smiled.

"What do you want if you're not here to fight?" Rae said, still not believing her.

"We're here to help Steve Holcomb," Julie replied as the others made a semicircle around Rae and Bobby.

Not lowering their hands, Bobby and Rae walked backward, thinking the others were going to trap them.

"You know Steve?" Rae questioned.

"Yes. I'm working at the facilities where he's being held."

"So you're the one who kidnapped him," Rae said angrily.

"No, no one kidnapped—"

"You're keeping him without his consent, so what's the difference?" Bobby interrupted.

Julie sensed that Bobby and Rae weren't going to relax. "Captain, I'm sure I'll be okay here by myself. They might be willing to listen if everyone else wasn't here."

"Captain?" Rae said. "So you guys are in the military?"

The others chuckled, and Julie said, "Not in the 'military' sense of the word you're accustomed to." She smiled at Bobby and Rae. "This is Captain Carson. I'm Lieutenant Miller, and I'm sure you remember Lieutenant Waters and Lieutenant Bell." She pointed to Sandy and James.

"Yes, I do. And I still have a bone to pick with you two, so don't go too far," Bobby said with some courage, pointing his finger at Sandy and James.

As the others started fading from view, Sandy walked up to Bobby. "Mr. Eriks," she said, smiling, lifting up her finger and causing Bobby to flinch. Then she blew him a kiss just as she vanished, leaving Rae and Bobby there with Julie.

"As I said, we are here to help Mr. Holcomb. And to help him, I'm going to need your cooperation," Julie said.

"Our cooperation?" Rae said, now feeling comfortable enough to walk over to the lieutenant.

Julie walked onto the pier to look at the pond. "It's nice here."

As Rae followed her, Rae said angrily, "We want our friend back and you guys out of our lives. That's the only cooperation you'll get from us."

"Right now, that's not possible," Julie said, looking sternly at Rae, and then glancing over to where Bobby was still standing. "I would like to meet with you two and Mr. Birch in reality. Is there some place where you would feel safe?"

Now it was Rae's and Bobby's turn to chuckle at the lieutenant. "We thought we were safe here," Bobby said, walking over to the bank of the pond.

"This was our safe place in reality and in dreams. But now, that's gone too," Rae spoke up, finishing Bobby's thoughts.

"No, Lieutenant, we can talk here," Rae said adamantly.

"Besides, we can't find David in dreams, and we haven't been able to get hold of him in reality," Bobby said, still looking at the water.

"I'm starting to think you guys also have David," Rae told the lieutenant.

Julie gave a few explanations as to what might have happened, but none of them seemed to go over too well with Bobby and Rae. "Miss Woods, I'm in town, and having some place to meet in reality would make it easier and more private," Julie said, trying to get Rae to change her mind. Rae just stood there and stared her down. "Very well," the lieutenant said, as she stretched out her hand. "At least let's be comfortable." She smiled when a table and three chairs appeared on the grass.

"So how can we help Steve?" Bobby said as he changed a hard chair into a much softer one before sitting down.

Giving him a grin, Julie walked over and took a seat, and then Rae joined them. "First, I want to assure you, I truly am here to help Mr. Holcomb, but I need your complete honesty. Is that a deal?" the lieutenant said, looking at both Rae and Bobby. "Captain Carson and I can help Steve."

Bobby and Rae agreed to be honest until the time they didn't want to talk.

Lieutenant Miller started asking questions about them. She asked how they came to learn the gift of dreams, if there were others like them, and if they had the same gifts as Steve when it came to controlling reality.

They lied about Mary to ensure her safety but shared with Miller as much as they felt they could.

"Amazing," Julie said, sitting back in her chair with awe. "So what happened to Mr. Holcomb?" Lieutenant Miller asked.

Bobby told Miller that Steve had a hard time growing up, and he believed Steve got lost somewhere along the way when the dreams he thought he wanted weren't what reality was.

"Steve isn't a murderer, Lieutenant," Rae insisted.

"No, he's not. And that's why I'm here now, to prevent him from becoming one," Julie said.

"Did he cause that lady to shoot her husband?" Bobby asked.

"I'm not sure, but it seems that way. It happened not too long after Steve was brought into the facility. And ..." The lieutenant hesitated.

"And what?" Rae asked.

"And that's when I saw the note on the door of some house

where you guys were."

"So you've been spying on us," Rae said, abruptly standing up from the chair.

"It wasn't because we decided to spy on you. Until I met Mr. Holcomb, we didn't even know you existed. Miss Woods, please hear me out," the lieutenant pleaded as Rae paced back and forth.

"Fine," Rae said, and then a different chair, away from the table, appeared, and Rae sat down.

"Fair enough," Miller responded. She then told them she believed that Tillian was trying to use Steve's abilities to affect others for his own benefit.

"So why can't we get a hold of Steve now?" Bobby asked.

"I'm not sure why you can't reach him. I'm no longer able to reach his dream either." She looked over at Bobby with a concerned look. "Maybe he doesn't want us to find him. Or maybe it was someone else."

"No, I'm sure it's Steve," Rae said disappointedly.

"Miss Woods, Mr. Eriks, do you really believe both of you and Mr. Birch are the only ones who have this gift?"

"Apparently not. You're here," Rae snapped.

"There are others besides us," Julie said. "And I'm trying to protect you from those others. If it got out about your gift, they would eventually come after you."

Rae walked back over to the table and sat down on the chair the lieutenant created. "There are others?" Rae said, looking at Bobby.

"What can we do?" Bobby asked the lieutenant.

"You need to let us take you into protective custody." Julie replied.

"Shit!" Lieutenant Miller said as she watched Bobby and Rae fading.

Waking up naturally on the floor of the vacant house, Rae

and Bobby sat up, thinking about what Julie had just shared with them. "I'm not sure if we can trust her to let her take us into custody," Rae said.

"I wonder who the others are," Bobby said.

"You think Tillian is planning on using Steve to teach them about controlling reality?" Rae said gravely.

"I sure wish David was here to help," Bobby said.

Rae thought for a moment and then said, "Right now, there's only one person I think we can trust, and that's Detective Long."

CHAPTER 10 DREAMS

Rae and Bobby had contacted Detective Long and agreed to meet him at the restaurant where they had met after Suzie's dream. "We can't find David anywhere," Rae told the detective before she even sat down in the booth.

Looking at her with surprise, Detective Long said, "You haven't been in contact with his parents?"

"No. We've kept our phones off most of the time. We've been using someone else's," Bobby replied.

"David was in a car wreck a couple of nights ago," the detective spoke quietly.

"What? Is he okay? What happened?" Rae said, trying to catch her breath.

"A car ran into him; T-boned him pretty hard. He's in stable condition."

"What else?" Bobby asked after seeing the detective was about to say something more.

"He's in a coma," Long answered.

Unable to find any words, Rae just sat there staring down at the table, and her eyes started tearing up.

"Rae, I'm sure they didn't have anything to do with it. It was just an accident," Bobby said, trying to help her to get her mind off of what might have happened.

Detective Long didn't believe that it was just an accident. "Who are *they*?" he asked.

While Rae sat in silence, Bobby told Detective Long what had transpired since they'd met the last time and about last night's dream encounter with Miller and the others.

"So this Lieutenant Miller says there are others who have the ability to control reality?" the detective asked.

"We're not sure what they can do. We only know they can get into others' dreams," Bobby responded.

"We need to see David," Rae finally spoke up.

"Right now I don't think that would be very good idea," the detective said.

"And why not?" Rae spoke loudly in frustration.

Detective Long let Rae and Bobby know that right after the wreck, an Agent Collins was inquiring about the two of them and their connection with Steve. Since Long never contacted the FBI regarding money laundering, he believed Tillian must have sent the agent.

"If they did smash into David's car, can't you do anything about it?" Rae said, upset with the lack of help from Detective Long.

"I know it seems we're not doing anything, but believe me, Detective Yoder and I are doing what we can to ensure we find the person responsible for David's accident," Long said.

"Now what do we do?" Bobby said, feeling lost in their situation.

Detective Long asked more questions about Carson and Miller and the other Luciders.

After getting the information he needed and agreeing to help Bobby and Rae as best as he could, he told them to stay where they were and to not contact anyone except for him or Detective Yoder.

After getting back to his office and telling his partner what was going on, a woman interrupted him.

"Excuse me, Detective Long? I'm Lieutenant Julie Miller."

"How can I help you, Lieutenant Miller?" Detective Long looked surprised.

After a few days and some calls, Detective Long finally called Bobby and Rae to discuss a plan he and Detective Yoder came up with.

That night, Rae contacted Mary for any help she could provide in dreams. Rae, Bobby, and Mary were in the car in front of the hospital, watching the raindrops roll down the windows as they waited for Detective Long.

"Do you think their plan will work?" Rae asked.

"I'm not sure," Bobby admitted. "I just don't want David to end up like Steve."

"Me, too," Rae agreed. "It's 2:30 in the morning. Where are they?" Rae turned around to see Mary sleeping in the backseat.

"They're here," Bobby told her as a car pulled up next to them, just away from the parking lot light that shone around them. Approaching the car, detectives Long and Yoder went to the passenger side, and Rae rolled down her window.

"Are you ready for this?" Detective Long asked as he opened an umbrella for Rae.

"Ready as I'll ever be," she answered, and then she told Bobby, "You make sure you keep the car running."

Walking into the hospital, Detective Yoder handed Rae a bag, and then she went into the women's restroom. When she came out, she was wearing a nurse's uniform.

"Okay, let's see if we can get him," Long said as they headed toward the elevator to the third floor. They reached the room where an officer was sitting outside the door. Rae kept walking past him, not giving any indication she knew the detectives.

"How's he doing?" Detective Long inquired.

"I haven't heard a sound out of him," the on-duty officer replied.

"Has anyone been to see him?" Yoder questioned as he looked around the area.

"No, sir," the guard responded.

"Well, you take a break. Detective Yoder will keep watch," Detective Long said. "I want to check in on him."

"This late, sir?" the officer asked.

"Yes, this late. Is there a problem?" Detective Long responded severely to the officer.

"No, sir," the guard said and then took his break.

"Mike, once you go into that room, your job is on the line. I don't mind helping you; I just want to make sure one more time that this is what you're willing to do for someone you barely know," Dale Yoder said.

Mike smiled, opened the door, and went in.

Rae looked around to make sure the on-duty officer wasn't coming back. Then she grabbed a wheelchair and went into the room. She stood there, watching for any signs that Mary was in my dream.

As Mary floated slightly above the floor in the lotus yoga position in her dream house, a yellowish ball of flame appeared in front of her. It grew larger and finally stopped when it was about twelve inches in diameter. Mary tried to steady the fading scene that appeared in the flames. "David," Mary spoke quietly.

When she didn't get a response, she started chanting some words, trying to make the scenery clearer, and then suddenly, the scene changed and she saw me sitting in the cafeteria, talking with Steve. "David, can you hear me?" Mary questioned as she raised her voice louder. Then the ball of flames collapsed within itself, vanishing from view. Mary tried again, only to see me standing at the park before the ball of flames buckled again.

Just as she was about to try one more time, she heard a voice. "Hello, Mary." Setting her feet on the floor quickly, Mary looked to the woman who stood in the shadow of her dream.

"Who are you?" Mary asked.

The woman ignored Mary's question, saying, "It looks as if you could use an extra force to help you stabilize his dream." The woman came through the portal.

"How do you know my name, and what are you doing here?" Mary questioned, concerned for her safety.

Just as Mary's dream house started to fade, the woman said, "Mary, I can help you contact David." Sandy Waters pleaded for Mary to keep her dream going. Caught between being awake and asleep, Mary stood between both worlds, looking at Lieutenant Waters. "Mary, I can help you. Please let me," Sandy said softly. As Mary continued to stare at Lieutenant Waters, another fireball grew in the center of the room. "Thank you," Lieutenant Waters said as she sat down on the floor across from Mary.

As Sandy watched Mary hovering in the yoga position, staring into the ball, Mary started chanting words again. Sandy focused on bringing the scene into view, where Mary could see me standing at the pond. Mary started to dissolve and then vanished into the flaming ball of fire, leaving Sandy alone, watching the scene...

As Mary came closer to me, she smiled. "You sure are hard to get a hold of," she said sweetly. "We've been searching for you."

"Mary?" I wondered if it was truly Rae's little sister standing in front of me or just another delusion I was having.

"Yes, David, it's me," she replied, smiling with joy.

"What are you doing here?" I asked, not knowing why she would be coming from the woods.

She reached out to take my hand. "Let's go home," she said, trying to lead me.

I planted my feet and wouldn't follow. "Mary, what's going on?" I asked, as I looked around for others.

"David, this isn't real. This is only a dream, and you're having a hard time waking up from it."

"Mary, I'm sorry, but this is real. I thought I was dreaming at first. But when I go to sleep and wake up, it's still the same," I said, trying to convince her. As she stood there telling me that what I was seeing was not real, I started believing she wasn't real either. Maybe it was true. Maybe I'd reached the point where I couldn't tell reality from dreams any longer, and now everything around me was delusion.

Mary tried her best to persuade me that I was stuck inside a dream. "You were in a wreck," she said, starting to get frustrated with me.

"I'm sorry, Mary, but I would know if I'd been in a wreck." I felt strongly that this was a delusion.

"Okay, I tried it your way," she said with a laugh. "Now I'm gonna do it my way." She smiled a girlish smile.

In addition to Mary's ability to keep dreams going, she could also stop them immediately. But the problem with dreams being stopped quickly is that when a person doesn't wake up normally, he or she might get sick. Think of it this way: You're on a merry-go-round, going as fast as you can, and then, all of a sudden, you're standing still: Not a good feeling. In addition, Mary likes to use magic to enhance things and add drama to the things she does.

I told her to stop clowning around, but the last thing I remember seeing were balls of light coming from her hands, reaching into the sky. And the last thing I heard was her laughter as my dream and reality started clashing together.

Worlds within my dreams started spinning faster and faster as I stood in the middle of nowhere—but everywhere at the same time. Scenes from both dreams and reality encircled me to the point that I wasn't able to determine which was which. As each scene came into view and quickly left, lightning also

LUCID DREAMERS - THE LUCIDERS

followed, separating each vision I was having, which was then chased by a clap of thunder.

Storms passed overhead and the dark clouds drifted downward, overpowering the visions I saw. I stood in the rain, watching the lightning flashing in and around the clouds. The winds blew each vision into focus, and then I watched them shatter. Just as my mind was about to split in two, I heard a voice say, "She's doing it." It was Rae; she watched my eyes moving rapidly as my two worlds crashed into each other.

"David?" I heard Rae's voice somewhere in the distance of my mind, in between dreams and reality. "Come on, David, wake up." Her voice grew louder with each passing dream as it shattered into pieces from the weight of reality. Mary's laughter faded into the distance, as Rae's pleas for me to wake up got closer. As I leaned over the edge of the hospital bed and started vomiting onto the floor, I heard Rae's slight laugh of joy, and she helped bend me over farther to get the sickness out of me.

"I don't mean to sound insensitive, but we need to go," Detective Long said.

"What? Go where?" I asked, looking around the room, trying to determine where I was.

"David, you're in the hospital," Rae told me.

"Explain it to him later. Get him out of here now!" Mike spoke forcefully.

"David, no matter what happens, until we are in the car I don't want you to say a word. Okay?" Rae asked, and I heard the seriousness in her voice. "David?" she said again, as I seemed to be going in and out of consciousness.

"Sure." I heard myself sounding incoherent as Rae and the detective put me in the wheelchair.

Detective Long went out of the room first. "Okay, take him down the back elevators and head to the car," he said.

As Rae wheeled me down the hall, I faintly heard conversation behind me.

"Is he still out?" the officer asked, returning from his break.

"Actually, no. He's awake now," Detective Long said. Then he called after Rae, "Excuse me, nurse?"

As Rae looked back at Mike, she gave him an odd look.

"Sorry to bother you, but the gentleman in here has woken up, and he's in pain. Could you get him a pain pill?"

Rae stood there in disbelief. She didn't know what Detective Long was up to, but she played along. She left me in the middle of the hall, facing away from the officer, and headed back toward the room. Opening the door just a little, she poked her head inside. "Did you need a pain pill, Mr. Birch?" Rae asked an empty bed. "Okay, as soon as I get this patient back to his room, I'll be right back."

While Detective Yoder kept the officer busy, Rae shut the door behind her. "What the hell are you doing?" Rae whispered to Detective Long.

"Just get him out of here now," he replied.

Just as Rae and I disappeared down the hall, Agent Collins and another agent were coming from the front elevators.

"What are you doing here, Collins?" Detective Long asked the FBI agent. Cutting them off at the nurse's station, Mike asked again. "I said, what are you doing here?" He and Detective Yoder stood in the agent's way.

"We're here to check on the kid, and I would advise you to move, Detective," the agent said as he tried to move past Long and Yoder.

"No, you're not going to check in on him now," Detective Long said, pulling a paper out of his jacket. "This is an order from a judge to prevent anyone but his family, hospital staff, or me from going into the room until I can finish my investigation."

"You were taken off the investigation, as I recall," Collins said.

"So you're working with Colonel Tillian?" Detective Long asked, even though he knew that Tillian had taken the investigation away from him. When Collins didn't immediately respond, Detective Long said, "I'm investigating a hit-and-run that Birch was involved in, not the stolen car and money that you seem to know about."

"I believe Birch was somehow helping Holcomb, and that's what I plan on finding out," Collins replied.

"Now, you're more than welcome to go in there, but since this is a judge's order, I'm sure you will obey an order of the court, or I will have to arrest you. It's your decision."

Collins considered his options. "Officer, is he still in the room?" he asked, sounding disgusted.

"Yes, sir, in fact, the nurse is getting him a pain pill now," the officer said.

"So he's awake now?" Collins said, looking surprised. Not getting a response, Collins looked back at the nurse sitting at the station. "Excuse me, nurse, is the kid in the room awake?" Collins questioned her.

"Yes, sir. In fact, one of my nurses is looking after him," the head nurse replied.

"You know, all I have to do is make a phone call, and I will get the kid," the agent said to Detective Long.

"Yes, I'm sure you can, but until then, you won't get into the room," the detective assured the agent.

Collins turned to the other agent. "You stay here and make sure no one goes in or leaves that room, as our friendly detective suggests," Collins said. "I will be making that call." Agent Collins left the other agent to stand around the nurse's station.

The detectives disappeared down the hall, where they saw the head nurse.

"You two owe me. I haven't worked the graveyard shift in years," Dale Yoder's wife said as she smiled at the detectives.

"I'll buy you and Dale a steak dinner," Detective Long said, and then the detectives headed toward the elevator.

"Include lobster with that dinner!" Mrs. Yoder called after them.

"I sure hope you know what you're doing, Mike," Detective Yoder said as they rode the elevator down.

"I do too."

After telling Bobby to follow them, the detectives took off to an unknown location as I lay in the back of the car with Mary, who apparently also had gotten sick when she stopped the dream. When we stopped at a motel outside of town, Rae and Bobby helped me to the motel door.

"Dad! Is it really you?" I asked, as he stood in front of me when he opened the door. I felt relief and started to cry because he was alive, but my dad looked oddly at me as I stood there. I wiped the tears off my face and hugged him until my mom pried me away, laughing and smiling at the same time, and then she hugged me.

After giving my mom a hug, I found out that Tommy and Wendy were at home, unaware of what was going on, other than I was still in the hospital. I told my parents about the dream I'd had when I thought my dad was dead. And then we spent the remainder of the early morning hours talking about what had happened after the accident.

"You know they won't stop trying to find you?" Detective Long told us.

"So there's nothing we can do for these kids?" my dad questioned the detective angrily.

"Yes, there is, but they need to stay hidden for now."

"Why are you helping us?" I asked the detective.

"Suzie." Detective Long smiled. "No one has a right to control someone else's dream."

"So where are we going to go?" Bobby asked.

Detective Long gave Bobby a note with an address on it. "It's going to take you a couple of days to drive there," he told

Bobby, and then he told me there was a doctor who would give me a checkup.

"Are you serious?" my mom asked.

"Detective, what is going on that David and his friends need to leave?" my dad asked.

"I think it's best if the kids tell you," the detective said and then headed out to the car.

Rae spoke compassionately to her younger sister. "I need you to take care of Dad. He's going to need help understanding everything that happened."

"When do you think you'll be able to come back?" Mary asked as tears filled both her and Rae's eyes.

"I'm not sure. As long as we stay here, we all are in danger," Rae responded.

"I can come with you," Mary said, looking toward the rest of us.

"They don't know about you. Besides, we'll be in each other's dreams," Rae said, finally smiling at Mary.

As they gave each other a hug, Rae and Mary walked back to the rest of us. We all stood next to the detective's car, each of us giving Mary a hug good-bye. When it was my turn, I gazed at her with a warm smile, thinking what she had done for me. "Thank you, Mary, for helping me out of that nightmare. If it wasn't for you, I'm not sure how long I would still be in there." I hugged her harder.

"And you thought I couldn't help all this time?" she responded with a chuckle, trying to hide the sorrow she was feeling.

"If you need me, you know how to get me," I said to her and then smiled. Mike Long opened the back car door for Mary as she took one more look at us and climbed in the car.

"Rae, we'll watch out for her and your dad," my mom told Rae as she put an arm around her.

After getting in the car, Detective Yoder rolled down his window. "Good-bye and good luck." He pulled out of the parking spot and headed back toward town. As we stood in the street watching them leave, we could see Mary in the backseat of the car, waving good-bye. But we knew it wouldn't be long before we would see her again.

Although reality may be able to keep loved ones away from each other, at least in dreams they are always together, and it wouldn't be long before Mary's smile would be there with us.

"So are you kids going to tell us what is going on?" my dad said, looking at us seriously. Not knowing how to start, we did end up telling them everything. My mom and dad just sat there in awe as we finished telling them our story. "So until we know we're safe from Tillian and hopefully find a way to get to Steve, I don't know what else to do," I told my parents. Without saying a word, my mom started giving us hugs as her eyes watered up.

"Well, you kids are going to need this," my dad said and handed us money to help us get to where Detective Long suggested.

After saying good-bye and letting Bobby know they'd check in on his grandmother, they too left us standing in the parking lot of the motel. Once again we were alone and confused about what to do next. "Well, I guess we should be going," Bobby spoke up.

"Yeah," Rae and I agreed with him sadly, looking back at the road that took us home.

We didn't know what was going to happen as we left in opposite directions, but we knew at least for now, we needed to stay ahead of Tillian and Collins. We didn't know what had happened to Steve, other than what Miller had told Bobby and Rae, but each of us wanted to let him know we were sorry for betraying him as we did. But we also knew that if we had told the truth in the beginning, we would be where he was—in the government's hands.

"You son of a bitch!" Colonel Tillian stormed his way into Detective Long's office. He'd been notified by Collins I couldn't be found. "Where the hell is Birch?" Tillian shouted. "I want Birch now." He threw papers down on Mike's desk.

"I don't have him," the detective said.

"The hell you don't. When Collins got the injunction to go pick up the kid, he was gone. Now, I want him!" Tillian shouted again.

Mike's captain walked into Mike's office and said, "Someone want to explain to me what's going on?"

Tillian spoke loudly to the captain. "Yes, I will. This bastard let my prisoner go."

"How is Birch a prisoner when he was the one who got hit in the hit-and-run last week?" Detective Long said. "In fact, we were just running the plate numbers we got from a witness. The way I see it, and how the officers who witnessed the wreck explained it, is that the vehicle crashed into Birch's car on purpose. And when they turned on their sirens and headed that direction, the car left in a hurry, eluding them. So you tell me, how the hell is Birch a prisoner?" Detective Long got closer to Tillian's face. "And one more thing … as soon as I find the ass that ran into the kid, I will personally handle the matter."

Agent Collins had been standing there watching, and now Mike noticed him leaving his office as fast as he could. "I figured as much," Mike said, walking back to his desk.

"You have something to say, Detective?" Tillian questioned, also upset.

"Do you, Mike?" the captain also questioned.

"No, sir, I sure don't." Mike smiled as he responded.

"I figured as much!" Tillian mocked Detective Long's own comment. "Captain, here's official paperwork for me to take Birch into custody. Your detective here thought he could help him get away."

"Mike, is that true?" the captain inquired as he glanced at the papers Tillian threw on Mike's desk. "If you're helping this kid, it will cost you your job and turn into a case of aiding and abetting."

"What is Birch wanted for?" Mike asked.

"Just tell us where he is. I know you were at the hospital last night with him. So where is the kid?" Tillian demanded.

"I told you, I really don't know. I had a lead I was following up on. And I asked Judge Carlin to give me a restraining order to keep anyone from seeing Birch until I could follow up on this lead. Here's the judge's order, if you want to look at it," Mike told his captain.

"That expired this morning at 4:00," the captain said. He found it odd to have a time stamp on the order.

"Yeah. I guess since I couldn't keep anyone out of the room by law after 4:00, someone must have come by and picked him up," Mike said with a slight smile.

"An agent was there when you were and didn't leave until I got there this morning," Tillian said.

"I really can't help it if your man didn't stay awake on the job. The officer I had on duty was only obligated to stay there until four this morning," Mike said.

"The hell with you," Tillian said and stormed out of the office as Detective Yoder walked into Mike's office.

The captain looked at Yoder and asked, "I suppose you don't have a clue what's going on either?"

"About what?" Detective Yoder asked, surprised.

"That's what I figured," the captain said and left Mike's office.

After driving for a couple of days, we reached the address Detective Long had given Bobby. "What the hell?" Bobby said as we stopped in front of a gate where guards stood watching us. After asking about our business, a voice came over the guard's radio, telling him to let us pass. We drove up the long road and parked in front of a large house.

"Shit! That bastard turned us in," Rae said angrily as Lieutenant Miller walked down the porch, heading toward the car.

She tapped on the window until Bobby rolled it down. "Hello, Mr. Eriks, Miss Woods. And it's nice to see you too, Mr. Birch," she said, smiling. "Please step out of the car and follow me." She headed back to the porch. We were escorted by a couple of guards and then we were taken into an elevator.

Once we were sitting in a conference room with Miller, Carson, and a few others, Bobby spoke up. "Why are we here?"

"For your safety," Captain Carson said sternly as he looked at some paperwork.

"Our safety?" I asked.

"That's right, Mr. Birch," a man said as he came into the room.

"Senator Wilson, thanks for coming," Lieutenant Miller said.

"Sir, what are you doing here?" Captain Carson asked.

"So these are the kids," the senator said, smiling at us.

"Captain, if I may," the lieutenant said, and then explained to everyone in the room what was going on.

"Lieutenant Miller is correct in what she said," Senator Wilson told the group around the table. "I had thought it was just a normal dream, but after being contacted by the lieutenant, I knew then Tillian was behind it."

"Senator," said Captain Carson, "how are you involved in all of this?"

"I am on the committee that contrived the Dream Catcher project," the senator said. "There were two parts of the project: one was to determine if a person was able to control his or her dreams and the dreams of others. If the first part of the project was successful, we would start the second phase and find out if reality could be controlled by dreams." The senator also explained that two teams were part of the project, but were unaware of each other and that Colonel Tillian was in charge of one team, and a Colonel Miller had been in charge of the other, before he passed away.

"Your father?" Captain Carson asked Julie. She nodded, and the senator went on to explain that Colonel Miller's team had learned to control dreams.

"But, according to Tillian, his team was unsuccessful, and eventually, the men and women fell into a coma."

"A coma?" Lieutenant Waters asked the senator.

"Yes. Apparently, according to a Major Maiden, who was the psychiatrist for Tillian's side of the project, the team's memories of reality were being distorted. After an investigation, Captain Jacob's squad seemed to be okay and Tillian convinced the majority of the committee to continue the project. Soon after the project was restarted, that's when all the members went into a coma. I did have my suspicions, because the only drugs to be used were sedatives to help the team sleep longer, not warp their memories or even strong enough to induce a coma. So in order for the committee to get my vote to let the project continue, I asked that your psychiatrist, Lieutenant Miller, be assigned to Tillian's team, but with one condition—Lieutenant Miller had to learn to control her dreams."

"But sir, Julie was already able to control her dreams before she even started to work under Colonel Tillian," Sandy said, feeling confused.

"True, Lieutenant, but Tillian and the committee didn't know that. I had learned it from Colonel Miller, who was a very close friend of mine," the senator responded. "I figured if Tillian wasn't conveying everything to the committee as he was supposed to, then Miller, who already had the same knowledge as the team here, would take over, as the psychiatrist after Maiden was told to leave the project, and hopefully help me find out what Tillian was up to."

Lieutenant James asked, "If Colonel Tillian was using drugs other than sleeping pills in the experiments that ultimately put Captain Jacob and his team into a coma, why didn't the drugs affect Julie and put her into a coma?"

Lieutenant Miller spoke up. "Colonel Tillian didn't know I had learned dream control until much later. He knew I was to report directly to Senator Wilson and the committee. After he found out I could control dreams, he had me monitor the team and pass on orders, via dreams."

"So you're saying Captain Jacob's team, even though they are in a coma, are still dreaming, and you can talk to them?" Lieutenant Waters asked.

"Yes," Lieutenant Miller said.

"Damn, this shit is way out there." Lieutenant James spoke out of turn and then said sheepishly, "Sorry."

"Senator, if I may interject, are you suggesting that Colonel Tillian purposely put the other team in a coma?" Carson asked.

"I don't know. But I do know this, Tillian lied to us about his team's abilities, and I believe he's working on the second part of the project, which apparently this Holcomb kid already knows how to do," the senator said.

"So it was easier for him to take our friend, rather than try more experiments," I said.

"In a nutshell, yes," Lieutenant Miller answered for the senator. "One more thing, Senator, that even I'm not understanding," Lieutenant Miller spoke up again. "Why is the committee letting Colonel Tillian continue if they know the other team is still in a coma?"

"I really can't answer that. I've been trying to get the funding to stop since the incident a couple of years ago, but someone has been going to bat for Tillian, and I haven't been able to find out who is helping him."

"And why are we here?" Bobby spoke up again.

"To help us stop Tillian and get your friend back," Lieutenant Miller answered.

Over the next few days, while hiding somewhere in the countryside under the protection of Captain Carson, we sat at the pond, thinking that when—or if—we found Steve, we hoped he would forgive us for putting him into this mess. But as we sat there for the moment, enjoying our dreams without reality interfering, that's when Steve finally walked through a portal and stood in front of us.

As I said, this is our story. We have the ability to dream as we wanted to, and we learned that dreams are an important aspect of our lives—and of everyone's. We gained the knowledge that if we wanted something in life, we had to dream about it. It just wasn't going to happen for us, because dreams aren't only for one's sleep; they are at our core and make us who we are. We've also learned that with dreams, there comes a sacrifice—some large, such as losing a friend, and some not so huge but just as important.

Finally our graduation day came, and we were determined to go through with it. We all worked hard to get our diplomas, and we weren't about to let Tillian or anyone else stop us from achieving our goals. We stood there in our graduation gowns outside the school, waiting for our names to be called. We had some excitement in our lives, but now, we were graduating. We'd be out of high school for good, and we couldn't wait to get on with our lives and the dreams we shared.

The principal spoke each student's name, and he or she walked up to the stage. "Lori Ashley … Robert Beckman …" he said as the onlookers clapped their hands. And then, I heard my name. "David Birch." I looked out into the crowd and saw my dad, mom, Tommy, and Wendy as they clapped and shouted congratulations to me. "Bobby Eriks," the principal said out loud after a few more students' names had been called. Bobby's family also clapped and shouted for him when he walked across the stage.

Finally, the principal said, "Raelen Woods." Rae walked up to receive her diploma. As the cheering went on, she looked and saw her family. She watched her mom and dad kiss each other, knowing their daughter had accomplished something. Mary was screaming the loudest as she stood on her seat, trying to look over the heads of other spectators, just to see her big sister center stage.

In addition to realizing the importance of our graduation, we also learned that some of the sacrifices we make could hurt when we live with our dreams. We learned this while we slept very peacefully, as Mary brought us a cake with words on it that read "Congrats Rae, David, and Bobby—Graduation Class of 2011" in our dream.

About the Author

Roy Johnson was born September 19, 1962 in Fort Wayne, Indiana. Roy currently lives in Brandon, Florida, with his fiancée, Arlene. Roy enjoys motorcycles and diving. Roy was inspired to write *Lucid Dreamers* after having a lucid dream.